Stripping Down to the Bones

Merry Clark

ISBN: 0615798691
ISBN 13: 9780615798691
Library of Congress Control Number: 2013939313
Nature's Edge, Cassopolis, MI

1. FALLING CLOSE TO THE TREE

At fifteen I started swearing.
It was a man who pushed me to it.
And my dad who taught me how.

My father was a mad scientist. Not crazy mad, but angry mad, or perhaps his anger drove him crazy. Rebelling against everything, he argued incessantly with his Republican father, a radiologist in Sycamore, Illinois, who did quite well for himself after the war. My grandfather had piled up farmland, invested in agricultural companies, and then hired someone to manage it all. My father's mother was born on a farm near Macomb, Illinois, and my father had loved the trips to his grandparents' farm.

He had been pushed to excel academically, and he played the French horn as well. His older sister was somewhat put off as she watched him receive excessive accolades and attention, and a rift emerged between them that widened through the years.

Although he was expected to follow in his father's footsteps, my father had other plans, and he eventually came to despise conservatives of all stripes. His parents were racist, after all. Rather than taking the stuffed-shirt track, he preferred life outdoors on the Illinois prairie, with the butterfly collection to prove it. So instead of becoming a doctor, he opted for scientist, and headed to Berkeley in 1959 to earn a PhD in biochemistry.

He had just married my mother, who was his college sweetheart from St. Charles, Illinois. She was planning to teach English in Hayward, California. Those years in California were probably the best years of their lives, as I did not come along till 1965. By that point, they were in Boston, where my father was doing research at MIT. I still like to think I was a bi-coastal production, having been conceived in their minds in California and in the flesh in Massachusetts. Being the first-born garners special treatment, of course, and my first solid food was lobster.

Alas, this research stint came to an end, and my father then obtained a professorship at Notre Dame, in South Bend, Indiana. So I was pulled away from the intellectual, cultural, and economic possibilities of Boston and dragged, kicking and screaming, to the southwest corner of Michigan. My parents found a quaint, red brick house close to the state line, with apple, apricot, and mulberry trees in the backyard. My brothers were born soon after the move to Michigan. Looking back, I finally realized that's why I have blue blood and they don't—which explains everything, really.

After a few more years of institutional life, my father was chafing against being institutionalized, so he began combing the Michigan countryside for farmland. At last he found a 500 acre parcel and took out a mortgage in 1976. His father passed shortly thereafter, and after a big fight with the banks and his sister, he was able to transfer some of the Illinois land to Michigan for a total of 1800 acres. He then gladly quit his job at Notre Dame and became the salt of the Earth—a farmer. An *organic* farmer. And that's how it all began.

Oh yes, his mother swore that he was wasting his education, and while it is true that it doesn't take a PhD to run a plow, he could pronounce the words on the label of widely used pesticides and knew what they meant. Thus he determined that he would forego the use of these substances and go against the grain, so to speak. He decided to focus on raising cattle and just putting them out to pasture, feeding them very little grain at the end. And he threw in a soybean crop for diversity. The local farmers in backwoods southwestern Michigan ignored his lectures, rolled their eyes, and predicted the farm would fail without the requisite pesticides and corn-fed animals.

As I watched him step to the beat of his own drummer, even among the weeds that initially sprouted up above the soybeans, I took my cues from the offbeat rhythm as I danced in the abandoned cabin that was just far enough away from the old farmhouse. I would dance in the driveway after dinner in the summertime, and he would come out, cross his arms, shake his head, and proclaim, "All you want to do is play, play, play." Is there anything else? Living off the beaten track kept me blissfully isolated from mainstream society. If only I could have stayed that way.

As it turned out, mainstream society beat a track to my door. At twelve, I discovered the proverbial magazines under my father's mattress and came completely undone by what I saw. Thus, my dad, the scientist and sex fiend, felt obligated to explain the meaning of these unsettling images to me. Since he was never one for tact, I stood across the kitchen from him, near the doorway, in case I needed to make a quick getaway. Nearing baldness on top, with brown eyes that could bore a hole through a maple tree, my father leaned ever so nonchalantly against the sink, arms crossed over a dirty T-shirt and a pot belly, and methodically described the gory details in the most clinical way possible. He finished with a flourish by exclaiming how beautiful and miraculous it all was. I was appalled, to say the least. Where was Mom? It was just wrong. I left the room believing that sex was a man's domain, and women did not speak of such things.

Much to my horror, later that year, I began "developing", and wearing very loose blouses to hide it. My father was against something called a "training bra," while my mother argued that I needed support. I stood there watching this exchange and felt the blood leave my face. There was too much estrogen in the house for my dad to handle, I guess. I hated that bra too. The additional frontal padding just got in my way when I was running, dancing, and climbing trees.

It was even more maddening when the periods started too. It all compounded to cramp my style and become one big distraction.

In conflict over my bodily changes and also witnessing an extreme close-up of the battle of the sexes unfolding between my parents, I developed definite opinions regarding the ongoing war. My mother taught me that women needed to fight to be treated as equals with men, that there was something inherently unfair about the status of women throughout history. Judging from how often my father yelled at her, there was definitely something unfair about her status in her marriage, so I swore I would never become like her. I sided with her during their arguments, defending her against this obviously misogynistic foe.

There was even one heated exchange that ended with my father telling me that if I kept up with the song and dance bit, he couldn't see me as being qualified for anything except prostitution. I was about fifteen at the time. See, he had to keep everyone under his thumb; we were only pawns in his game of domination. It was as if he had children just so they would work for him. But there was no way I would let him suffocate me; I had to prevail over him any way I could until I gained my emancipation. Men were indeed the enemy, so I vowed I would never marry.

After buying the farm, we moved from a white, small town to a more "integrated" smaller town nearby when I entered high school. My friends from the white town felt sorry for me and told me that I was going to a scary place. The school was located along the route of the Underground Railroad, and the descendants of some of the first emancipated African Americans were still living in that town. My parents were decidedly liberal and liked the idea of sending their kids to an integrated rural school. I wasn't so sure initially. Shy and awkward at first, I eventually blended in and made friends with kids from both sides of the tracks.

I never had the guts to sit in the back of the bus with the bad boys, being known as a "nice girl"—a dreaded label if you wanted to be part of the in crowd. There was this stuck-up blond girl who got on the bus after me, and I would watch her sit sideways in her seat, batting her eyes at the right times, fixing her Farrah Fawcett hairstyle, and putting on yet another coat of mascara like she was getting ready for the Homecoming Parade. For some reason, she and I never became best buddies. Besides, I was too distracted by my nervousness around the boys, being at once attracted to, afraid of, and repelled by the opposite sex. Sinking down in my seat, I buried my nose in a book or meditated on the wind blowing through the trees. Then I would try to render infinity into words. Emotions just drying up and blowing away seemed tragic to me. There had to be a way to capture them. So I chased after the wind. And due to the nature of the wind, I had my work cut out for me.

Running and biking long distances became what I did to avoid being trapped in the house with my family, and I did it every day, year-round, running or pedaling farther and farther away. The road beckoned me onward, and there was always a new route to investigate. While my two brothers were out in the fields, learning about planters, plows, and cattle, I was perpetually planning my next escape. They tried to bike with me a few times at my coaxing, but they always turned back while I kept going and going. Out there on an organic island, music and books became my world, as singers and authors existed on a higher plane and were much better company than anyone I knew, even in the abstract.

My need to run away led me into track during my freshman and sophomore years. Every day starting in March, the track team would gather, composed of the fast black girls, the super jocks, and the distance runners. I was the only girl who actually ran the nine miles around the adjacent lake with the few boys who could handle that distance. They were all two years older than I was. Thirty years later, I biked around that same lake with a seventy-six-year-old billionaire. I just barely beat him. His girlfriend turned around.

The cliques in that little high school of around five hundred consisted of the jocks, the cheerleaders, the geeks, the populars, the farm boys, and the misfits. So lunch was usually an apple sitting outside the door of the school. The food was not good, picking which crowd to sit with was impossible, and of course, I was always trying to lose weight. I wound up being a cheerleader, but only befriending one of them. I dated a very conceited senior geek at one point, went out a few horrible times with a football player, and hung out with a handful of the misfits who were kind of crossover geeks.

At that time and in that area, there was not much drug use—at least none that I knew about, but that's not saying much. The football player on whom I had a terrible crush may have known much more about this, but like I said, I was a "nice" girl, not someone who would get in on something like that. He was very cute though: sandy hair, mischievous blue eyes, in prime condition, and well—just a player, of course.

Yes, I was a cheerleader—Yay!! Go team go!! It was a girly thing to be, yet sort of athletic, and it made me feel like I belonged, somehow. Plus, there were the very stylish blue-and-white uniforms to twirl around in. That was not enough for me though; I also squeezed the pom-pom squad into my maniacal mix of extracurriculars, which was rather bold of me, since the pom-pom squad was all black girls. Yet they accepted me and even let me choreograph whole routines and do my solo spinning in the middle of it. That was my specialty: spinning to a fast beat and then regaining my equilibrium immediately. So impressive. Pretty crazy they were. Or I was.

It was the early eighties and such tremendous hits were out, such as "Fame" and "What a Feeling" and, along with the onset of *MTV,* the Madonna and Michael Jackson rage. I relentlessly practiced the choreography from "Thriller". The song "Maniac" from the *Flashdance* soundtrack became part of my daily dance routine in the cabin. But Mozart was there too. Both seemed quite fitting.

The group of misfit/geeks became the theater gang, and we performed in a few major works as *A Midsummer Night's Dream*, *Annie Get Your Gun,* and *Whose Life Is It Anyway?* Shakespeare had never been done in that town, but we pulled it off with rave reviews. The little troupe of thespians became my clan, and that's where I met my high school sweetheart. He was into chivalry: he wanted to be an actor and was drawn to Camelot, the Renaissance, et al. But his chivalry came across as chauvinism to me. Looking at me with deer eyes and a clownish face, he didn't understand why I didn't want him to carry my books or open my locker for me.

What was so hard to understand? Was I not perfectly capable of doing those things for myself? I wasn't one of those overly feminine and precious girls who enjoyed having men do everything for them and being protective and all that crap. Considering myself on equal terms with any man, I did not see why he should be overburdened while I was empty-handed. No strong woman can pretend to be helpless.

He never pressured me into any sexual acts, and I was far too repressed to even venture toward any unmentionable regions. We would just do some soft-core making out. In the midst of one of our sessions, he whispered, "Marry me. Let's spend the rest of our lives together." I just figured he liked making dramatic statements for effect. After all, he was an actor. In 1984, he went off to New York City, and I entered the University of Michigan.

2. UPROOTED

The shock of going from a small town to a huge university sets in place an insecurity complex that never really goes away. My own small, timid voice was drowned out by a cacophony of other voices, many of which seemed to know more than I did. Everyone was a valedictorian from a much larger school. It seemed I could only hear myself again when I was with the trees, the fields, and the wind. I knew I had to conquer my fears and eventually take on the world because I grew up in these wide-open spaces, yet such a sense of freedom and possibility brought with it problems with boundaries and authority. Pretension and superficiality were alien to me; only the pure and authentic would do. Such transparency does not usually lead to job security—or many friendships, for that matter. I wanted only to seek the truth and to tell the truth, with no agenda and no oversight. Anything else seemed pointless.

Getting squeezed into a dorm room with a Catholic pothead from Ohio and a spoiled Jewish girl from that uppity prep school in Bloomfield Hills made me long for my own space, for solitude. So night after night I roamed the campus, searching for my separate peace. I found it in the dance building. Almost every night around ten, after doing all my studying, I would drag my "boom box" across campus and try to sneak into one of the studios. Finding an empty studio was like spying a $100 bill on the sidewalk. Like an ecstatic bird, drunk on the wind, I would dance till midnight and then write in my journal until I fell asleep on the studio floor. The janitors would come in and mop me up. Then I would drag myself back to that cramped dorm room, hide my boom box, and climb into my top bunk, trying not to wake the princess below me.

One night, the stuffy chairman of the department caught me in one of the studios and proclaimed that the dance studios were reserved for dance majors only and therefore I was not allowed to be there. This was devastating; he couldn't possibly understand what that space meant to me. So I continued my clandestine visits anyway, attempting invisibility. Finally, one of the professors heard about me, and when he found me there, he invited me to take his class. Thus began my routine of sprinting from my Spanish class to catch half of his dance class. I wanted to learn a different language, and suffice it to say that I never became fluent in Spanish. But this new language of dance turned out to be far more difficult than I had ever expected. Not only was my technique almost nonexistent, I also had a different body type than the other girls, having curves where they had bones. In spite of all this, the professor encouraged me to audition for the department, competing against girls who had been in ballet class since the age of two. Dance was never something I "studied" in "class". It was just me, a wild creature spinning out of control, not knowing what I would do until I had already done it.

My academic studies were not neglected, however; I was fully academic for the first two years at Michigan and did well enough to be accepted into the Honor Society. But I needed space and movement. The classrooms were crowded, the dorm room was dinky, and I required music. There was still a pervading sense of alienation, of not belonging. Drinking was a river of socialization into which I never stuck a toe, and I had no group affiliation, plus I was from a town that no one had ever heard of.

After my brother also got accepted to Michigan, he could not (or decided he could not) make the leap from the small town to the big university, and he ran back home after one semester. My parents thought I didn't help him acclimate, but I did what I could, being as busy as I was, and I certainly did not have time for babysitting and coddling. It was reminiscent of when I would bike for miles and my brothers would turn around. I was determined to keep going no matter what, because I had decided that running back home was not an option, as my father was there.

At the audition, I used the music to spill my heart out, transforming into a wild Jackson Pollock of movement. The department chair was "flabbergasted" at my intensity. The faculty was stunned at my innovative "choreography", which I admitted I had just made up as I went along. Strangely enough, this impressed them even more. And so, out of the hundred or so girls who auditioned, I was one of the ten they chose. As overwhelmed as I was with the plethora of possible pathways at Michigan, I took the plunge into dance, thinking that I could pursue more sedentary fields later in life. Besides, people who were versed in this art form had chosen me to be part of it. Robert Frost would have been proud.

That was how I wound up spending most of my years at the University of Michigan sequestered in a dance studio. I was so attached to the place and so sure that I had to be there almost eighteen hours a day (as if just by being there my body and technique would change), I had no social life whatsoever throughout my college years. And my parents kept scaring me about sex and drinking. My father was a teetotaler who would have disowned me if he caught me with so much as a wine cooler. But it went deeper than that. It was fear: fear of not measuring up, fear of my own sexuality—and fear of men.

Late one night, I was stretching alone at the ballet barre when a fellow appeared at the door of the studio. Instantly conscious of my bright-orange tights, I froze in place and then tried to act like I didn't care. He seemed pleasantly surprised to see me there and said he was looking for the recreation building. Drawn toward the bright legs, he made his way closer to me as I tried to orient him to his locale, while continuing to stretch. He admired my flexibility, and it didn't take him long to ask me out. This made me nervous, but I felt I should accept, even though I didn't feel comfortable with this stranger. I could sense his lust without really knowing that's what it was. We agreed on a set time to meet again at the same studio.

When the time came, I realized I was afraid of him. After all, he was a strange man—the enemy. I waited in my dorm room until well after the meeting time and then went to the studio in the recreation building, which was a bit foolish, since anyone could look in the window there. But I thought it was late enough and the coast would be clear.

Sure enough, after a few minutes, I glanced over and caught sight of his furious face pressed against the glass. He took off toward the door of the building, and I grabbed my unfortunately hefty boom box and raced down the hallway into the twisting caverns of the building. He was in hot pursuit as we ran past people in the hallway, but no one seemed to take any notice.

Luckily, I knew secret passages. I pushed my way through the women's locker room and into the pool area and looked behind me. I didn't see him. I slipped through the door between the pool and the dance building, and kept on running, snaking my way through the studio caverns.

Like a hunted animal, I desperately sought a hiding place.

I went for the locker room, locked the door, and hid in a stall, standing on the toilet and holding my breath as I heard him rattling the door and yelling, "I know you're in there!" Then he somehow got a janitor to *unlock* the door for him!

I still have no idea what he said to the guy. I was sure at the very least he would rape me.

He burst in. I stayed put. He yanked open the stall door and found me standing frozen on the toilet seat, still clutching my huge stereo like a shield.

"Why did you run from me? Why did you blow me off?" he demanded.

"I—I don't know. I'm afraid of you." I didn't move.

"You need to grow up. You need mental help. I've never been so insulted."

I just stared at him, frozen. He stalked out and slammed the door. I never even told my mother about this, let alone anyone else. I was only nineteen. From then on, until the age of twenty-three, I lived like a nun in a dance studio convent, pouring all my sexual energy and passion into dance.

During my last semester, I taught aerobics at the gym near the mall and immediately met four men. By that time, I could sense that my sex drive was not going to stay in the closet much longer. Could these men all sense that I was a virgin—like moths to the flame? One of them came to one of my dance performances and was there waiting for me outside the door of the green room, wearing a suit and tie with a boutonniere. He'd even brought flowers. I was riding high in a black velvet jacket, lace blouse, and black polyester mini-skirt. Were both of us hoping to get lucky? He met one of my dance professors, and with a wink, she said, "Oh, so you're Mandy's beau. I always check out the men my students are seeing." I so admired her style.

We verged on getting lucky that night, but I was still too green to go all the way. And that was it for him, as a self-described "hardliner."

3. CRIMES

The spring before I graduated, I met a fellow fitness fanatic at the gym, and he had the physique to prove it. Jim worked in membership and noticed me the first time I walked in—bundled in a pink, quilted coat with the hood up. He started asking other employees about me. And he watched me teach my class. Eventually we started talking, and he showed me the proper way to use some of the exercise equipment. I found out he was thirty-three and had a daughter but had never been married. Not a problem, I thought. He was blond and built, with a smile to die for. I showed him a tape of one of my dance solos, and he was genuinely moved. We fell in love over a period of a few weeks.

When I told my dad I was in love with a thirty-three-year-old guy who had a daughter out of wedlock, it went over like a stale pizza. He thought I should wait till I found someone *younger* than me who was still a *virgin*. Whoever heard of a male virgin anyway? Why would I—a totally clueless female—want to be with someone else who was equally clueless? I wanted someone who was mature and knew what he wanted out of life. Mom and Dad were virgins when they got married at twenty-three. Sure, if you marry that young, it's possible. What if they hadn't married right out of college?

Jim told me it would take a strong woman to deal with the fact that he had a child. Why should I have had a problem with that? Lots of people have kids without being married. It could be said that raising a kid is easier than managing a marriage.

"Young women like you have a lot of power," he told me. "Just don't hurt me."

I should have been saying that to him. He had a job and a van, which represented power and resources to me. I wanted to be equal somehow. He wanted us to be a team. I was fine with any arrangement, as long as he didn't try to control me.

How much freedom would I have to give up to be in a relationship? What did I have to give up to be free? Could I still be "free," in every sense of the idea, while in a committed relationship? According to Jim, if a relationship is good, it should make both parties better. But what did "better" mean?

It was the first real relationship I'd had since high school. Ann Arbor was racy compared to the farm. No one, until Jim, had ever even mentioned sex to me since Dad freaked me out with his version of the birds and the bees. Now Jim was telling me that I should just know what to do instinctively. Was it my fault I was sexually inexperienced? He tried to convince me that I was being a prude and that there was nothing morally wrong with oral sex. The mere notion of that…stuff going down my throat. Slimy. Sex would make me older, and that was unthinkable. I saw myself as a temple. How could I allow a foreign being inside?

He saw the whining psycho I could be. And I saw a side of him that couldn't accept me as I was. How could we go on if I couldn't meet his needs? Maybe pairing the experienced with the inexperienced wasn't such a good idea after all. I would always feel like he was trying to dominate me, and like I was always the one with the neurotic hang-ups.

I had to endure those last days in my dinky apartment, survive my mood swings, finally graduate, audition for graduate schools, make money that summer, try to fulfill Jim's needs as fully as I could, stay young forever, dance forever, reach my full potential (whatever that was), and stop thinking that society was out to get me.

One day we picked up his daughter, Jessica, at her mother's mobile home to take her to the arboretum. Jim went in and Jessica came out—all set to go with her basket and doll. She jumped down the steps, sat down, and pet the dog for a moment, then got impatient, stood up, and looked back at the door. She gazed downward for a moment, probably hearing them argue inside. That's when I got this sinking feeling.... She stomped up the steps and looked in. Jim finally came out. Her mother never showed her face; she just closed the door behind him.

Off we went to the arboretum, with the dog in tow. Jessica was perched on his shoulders, and the sunlight was shining down on their faces and glinting off their blond hair. When she came down off his shoulders, she started running down a hill and promptly fell into the mud. She kept going off the path, singing, and making sounds that went along with the rhythm of her feet. She could be a performer someday, I thought, with her bright face, sprightly attitude, sense of rhythm...*Oh God, he has a daughter!* I hadn't fully comprehended it until that moment. I didn't even fully grasp the concept of having a child. What did it mean? How did it feel? They looked so much alike. They belonged together.

So I knew I was actually making his life more difficult. Maybe the most selfless, loving thing I could have done for him was walk away. He had probably spent close to $1000 on me already, and that was insane. How could I ever repay him? My whole future hung in the balance. Grad schools and Jessica had control; they were pulling Jim and me apart.

Recurrent nightmares invaded my sleep. I was stuck inside a vehicle while Jim and Jessica were just outside the window. I was knocking frantically and calling his name, but he was ignoring me and looking at her. When I finally could reach out to her, she turned into a snarling, black animal. Everything disintegrated, and all I could do was sputter some protests at having everything precious to me taken away. Then there was a flash flood of muddy water. After being jolted awake with the sensation of drowning, I ran outside to breathe.

Ultimately Jim got impatient with my neuroses and fear of losing my virginity, and I became resentful of him telling me that sex didn't hurt, or at least wouldn't once I started doing it. He didn't know anything about how I felt. To him, my expressing any of my doubts was whining. We couldn't make each other happy. I thought I could get along just fine without him. I could get a job and a cheap place; I wasn't picky. And *go* to grad school next year.

While I was still wrangling around with Jim, I met Drew, another actor. We met while I was doing backstage work on a musical. After we spent a night together (still without intercourse), I knew I couldn't live with Jim if it meant I couldn't see Drew. I still needed to be free. My dream of dancing had brought me so far, it had to be my first priority. I needed to find out what I could do on my own artistically in another part of the country.

Jim's possessiveness coupled with my honesty meant the end for us. After we had our falling out, I bicycled in tears to his apartment building to sit on the sidewalk and wait to catch him when he came home, hoping for a second chance. On the way there, I ran into Tim. Tim was a postman with sandy hair and a cute smile who delivered the mail to the health-food deli where I worked, and he also frequented the gym. He could tell I was upset, so I filled him in on what had happened. Then I continued on my way.

I waited hours for Jim, wearing my new summer dress and losing hope by the minute. But the thought of Tim kept popping into my head as well, and I found I wanted to "run into" him again—and soon.

It was almost ten when I finally gave up, trudged over to my bike, and slowly pedaled home. At least I had someone else to keep my mind distracted.

Over the next few months, I saw Jim from a distance at the gym from time to time—talking to someone else. One rainy day, my bike blew a tire, and I had to leave it locked to a sign. I hopped a bus and then got soaked walking the rest of the way to the gym. After I taught my one class for ten bucks, I began the rainy trek back home. He drove by in his van, saw me, and slowly pulled over to give me a ride, although he was none too obliging. We rode along in stony silence for about two minutes.

"Are you happy?" I asked.

"I'm trying." He sighed.

"What can I do for you?"

"Be happy. Go on with your life."

"Do I have a choice?"

"You always have choices. And you're making them."

"You have no idea how painful this is for me." I sniffled.

He sighed and then hardened. "Look, your pain is just a thorn in my side. You're not worthy of me now."

I had broken his rules.

"Are we over forever?"

"Nothing is forever."

We went to get the bike, and the cops came along and thought we were trying to steal it. So he started thinking trouble followed me wherever I went, and I was starting to think that too. I was living on the edge, and it seemed there was always some danger lurking in the bushes. Was it just because I was a woman that I felt so vulnerable?

As far as Tim went, he was gentler and less possessive. I was almost twenty-four by then, so the whole virginity thing was just getting old like I was. It was time to find out what sex was like, so I made a conscious choice to go ahead and do it with Tim. He didn't have to get me drunk; I just told him I was ready to try it. We were at his house in the middle of a sultry day in August, which made me feel a whole lot naughtier about the whole thing. The wild woman was emerging.

He started testing the nerve endings down there to see how responsive I was. He would touch something, look up at me, and ask, "How does that feel?" I would say, "Good," and squirm uncomfortably. It wasn't at all romantic and felt rather like a science experiment.

"Too clinical?"

"Yeah, I guess."

He crawled on top of me and we kissed and he worked on me...and worked on me. By the time he put on a condom, I was in a cold sweat. The process of penetration had me wincing and tensing every muscle in my body. Once he finally got inside, he did what naturally follows.

"Don't move!" I yelped in anguish.

"You have to move."

"Why?"

"Because you need friction or else nothing happens."

He tried to make the necessary maneuvers, but when he saw my pinched face, he pulled out. We both lay there panting for a moment.

"I'm sorry. You've probably been with much more experienced girls."

"Don't be sorry. You just need to relax; you're way tense. Next time we should drink some wine."

4. DISTANCE

After getting accepted to the University of Colorado in Boulder and getting fired from the health-food store for not wrapping up the cheese, I left Ann Arbor. After much wrangling with Dad about what sense there was in an MFA in dance and moving halfway across the country, I finally convinced my mother to drive me out to Boulder in mid-September. I would have to wait a year and a half to gain residency status before I could even afford to go to school in Colorado. No matter. I had to get out of Michigan somehow.

Mom helped me locate a room in a townhouse. She paid the security deposit to a geeky business-school type whose dad owned the place. After we had breakfast together, she hugged me in the parking lot and started crying. "You're too young to be so far away." I tried to console her while ignoring my own trepidation at the prospect of being so alone and far from home. Yet there was also a sense of possibility. The mountains were magical.

After she drove away, I stood in awe of where I was. Then I grabbed my bike and found the nearest entrance to the bike path. I pedaled east and west and north and south that day, without ever converging with automobiles. It gave me such a sense of boundless freedom that standing still felt like death. So I stayed in high gear, trying to live up to such a majestic backdrop.

Two months after being dropped off in Boulder, I had three jobs at two establishments: aerobics and childcare at the YMCA, and working a part-time night shift at Hardee's. Such is the life of the newly minted BFA. I saw myself as an underprivileged underdog—sometimes stealing food just to survive. These types of jobs were necessary, practical, and unavoidable, I told myself, but my patience wore thin within months. It's the restless souls who are apt to do almost anything to avoid a mundane life.

By the time the holidays came around, I was getting pretty lonely in provincial Boulder. One night I was teaching my aerobics class and a tall, lanky guy walked in and introduced himself. He was one of two guys in the class and didn't exactly fit in. He must have heard about a cute, young, flexible chick teaching a class at the Y, because I don't think he had ever taken a fitness class in his life.

I just did the normal things I had always done in dance class, but the image of me sitting with my legs splayed at three and nine, leaning forward with my chest flat on the floor, is perceived quite differently by a straight man than it is by other dancers in a dance class.

Jake was a beanpole thin, thirty-something Wyoming man with big green eyes; one of the original hippie techies of the Silicon Mountains, complete with the ponytail. He lived in a cabin up Flagstaff Mountain—a gorgeous thirty-minute drive (if you're good) from town. And he drove it every day in his Toyota truck to his tech job. He actually had a license plate that read MTNLVN. Living or loving? Both. We had a few dates and then I agreed to see his place in the mountains, trusting my emerging instincts that I would not wind up dead along some mountain pass.

The first night I rode up with him and saw the bright lights of Denver come into view over the ridge, I was forever hooked on the Front Range of Colorado. We wound our way up and down and around the switchbacks, up to seven thousand feet. As I watched him from the passenger's side, he seemed pleased to be able to share the ride and the experience of his place with me. Initially, I fell in love more with the mountains and his place than with him. It was a cabin after all, not unlike the one back on the farm. It was nestled along a dirt road with only a few neighbors, blending in with the pines.

The mountains seemed like just the place for him to go to become a hermit after his divorce from a woman he had met overseas as an exchange student. They had been living in Longmont, and she had been pregnant when she got tremendously homesick. So he wound up coming home from work one day around Christmas and found the house dark and empty. It was clear he had not recovered from this loss, as he was openly anti-remarriage.

He treated me nicely enough, and he enjoyed introducing me to all kinds of new experiences that clean-cut young girls from rural Michigan would not know much about, like waterbeds, wine, and take 'n' bake pizza. He had an old German shepherd who would go on hikes with us even though he had hip dysplasia. The only picture I have of myself in the mountains was taken by him at about ten thousand feet, with the Continental Divide in the distance. It was a brief trip to heaven.

By that time, I was sick of living with the anal retentives I had been tolerating in the townhouse, but I didn't move in with him. No, he had an ex-pseudo-girlfriend, Karen, who needed a roommate, and he introduced us. She was a singer, and we hit it off. He helped me move into the cozy apartment she shared with her son. My room came furnished with a dresser and a wooden frame for my mattress. It was nice to finally sleep up off the floor. Jake tried to at least be helpful to the women in his life, and maybe he secretly felt like he was creating his own harem. According to Karen, this was not that far from the truth.

Distance was built into the relationship from the start, so as I pushed for more commitment and closeness, he backed away. The last straw was when he invited both of us to his place for a barbecue in June. We went just because we liked his place and wanted to try to have fun. But he had also invited other CU students—mostly girls, younger than us.

I watched him through the smoke from the barbecue grill, chatting it up with yet another cute, young quarry. When I saw her, I saw myself. Their figures outlined a stark realization. His true intention was to share as many sexual peaks with as many young women as possible. He could hide the truth from himself, but he couldn't look me in the eye. Before I left, I warned her about him. Could he blame me?

A few weeks later, I decided to place a personal ad, in an effort to erase the pain with the distraction of others.

5. BY THE NUMBERS

The ad read:

"Creative and energetic Boulder woman
seeks strong/sensitive man for friendship/LTR."

After many lunch dates with various lackluster candidates, I had almost given up. As I waited in a café on Pearl Street for an older guy with a strange name, dressed like a grad student in transition, I told myself this would be the last loser I would wait for. Just then, a blond gentleman in a dark-blue suit and shades strode through the door. He looked at me through his shades and seemed to recognize me. He took them off and grinned, blue eyes glinting like chrome.

"Are you Mandy?"

"Yes," I grinned nervously. "You must be Steve."

He leaned over to hug me as soon as names were out of the way. And attraction was triggered at that very second. How do I say this without sounding like a bad romance novel? The man was magnetic, the center of the Earth without having to raise an eyebrow. We gravitated to a table, and he pulled out a chair for me. After we ordered, he proceeded to direct the conversation in the powerful manner at which certain men of stature seem to excel.

At the age of thirty-eight, he was divorced with no children. He told me they had married too young and their lives changed during the marriage. Steve liked change and wanted to grow in new directions. He was a genius with cars as well as computers. "I chose computers," he said, "because it's one field that would allow me to maintain my freedom of mobility. I'm also very interested in audiovisual work."

He shifted uncomfortably in his suit, glanced around, and added sheepishly, "I'm sorry I wore a suit. It's really not me. I'd wear a sweatshirt and jeans to work, but the people I work with aren't like the people on Pearl Street in Boulder." He grinned.

The conversation continued unabated for hours as we picked at our lunch and entertained obvious subtexts on both sides of the table. When I spoke, he was so attuned to what I said that I looked around for a hidden camera. He never gave up eye contact, never glanced about the room, at other people, or at his watch. It was what he said, how he said it, and how he looked at me when he said it. It was the leading questions, the pointed responses, and the intensity of his need to melt the layers of my personal shields. He was disarming me. His manner felt organic, yet all the right words came on cue.

After apologizing for being in a "business mode," he honored me with his business card. We donned our shades, and I floated back to my bike.

Friday night I went over my list of those who had made it through the first round. Out of the seventy or so I had interviewed, I easily whittled the crowd down to five. One in particular stood out: the handsome older gentleman in shades who had seemed genuinely interested in what I had to say.

"Hello, Steve? It's Mandy. Hi, um, we met on Thursday." My voice cracked a bit.

"Oh hi! Good to hear from you again! What are you up to?"

"Well, I was just considering who to call back, and your name floated to the top."

"Really? I'm flattered. This is a very pleasant surprise. I was planning on calling you this week, but I wasn't sure how you felt about me."

"Well, you're just about the only man out of seventy I've met so far who actually knew how to communicate."

"*Seventy?!* That many, huh? You've been busy this summer." He chuckled. "Well, I know I didn't act like it, but I was attracted to you when I first saw you. I'm just sort of...cautious. This is pretty gutsy of you, asking out an older man."

"Who says I'm asking you out? I'm just calling to talk." I claimed.

"OK. Then I'm asking you out. How about Sunday?"

That Sunday we went for Chinese. During the meal, the temperature rose steadily, ratcheted up by the Volcano we shared. He started the relationship talk.

"It's been a while since I've been in a relationship. I'm very selective, and I've been so busy with work lately. I'm trying to find some time to relax."

"Yeah, I know what you mean. It seems like I engineer a schedule for myself that doesn't include either rest or spare time. I'm a self-initiated workaholic."

"It looks like we can both start with a clean slate."

"Well, actually, I just ended another relationship. He was a cold man, also divorced, and he lives up in the mountains like a hermit. I tried to bike all the way up to his place once, got lost, and...oh hell, it's not important."

I kicked myself for giving away too much too soon.

"Yes it is, Mandy. You obviously need to talk about it. Please go on." His interest increased my interest as I felt heat spreading throughout my body, and then there was the inadvertent brush against his leg under the table. Looking him in the eye for more than a few seconds was impossible, even though he kept his eyes glued on mine. My gaze darted about the room while I toyed with my food and fiddled with the chopsticks I did not know how to use. Rambling on about my recent experiences in the big city of Boulder and my small-town beginnings, and musing about what the future might hold, I must have come across as quite the naïve little girl.

But this time around, I refused to feel pressured into anything, because I knew there was always someone else right around the corner. No more emotional prisons—I would call the shots and dole out the justice. Steve was just the "older man" I needed to explore a relationship with—as a learning experience, if nothing else. It was a novel idea: to feel liberated enough to be *myself* with an older man. That sense of liberation was attractive to me in and of itself; I just didn't want him to go around thinking he had it made, even if he did. But how could I decide if I really trusted this man? Did the attraction override underlying doubts?

We had dinner a few more times before I agreed to visit his place. Still having no car, I had to let him drive. This was becoming irksome to me as I was beginning to feel an aversion toward riding in the passenger's seat. But he drove a comfy Buick Riviera with an amazing sound system, so that made it easier to tolerate.

We pulled into the driveway of an unassuming house in a suburb of Denver. He shared it with his sister; she had the upper level, and he had the den. The first thing I noticed was that all the furniture was white. His sister met me with a clipped warmth and then quickly retreated to her room.

Downstairs he invited me to get comfortable in the small (white) living area and turned on the stereo. Toni Childs was one of his favorites, along with Seal. He then disappeared into his study, where he had an up-to-the-minute computer. The lilting voices transported me into an otherworldly, trance-like state. After he finished whatever it was he was working on, he came back to the sofa to find me nodding off. He came around to face me, got on his knees, and watched me till I woke up with the sensation of being watched.

"Are you sleepy, by any chance?" He laughed.

"Oh sorry. Um, yes, I guess so." I yawned and smiled shyly.

"Well, let's move you to a more comfortable place for sleeping."

He scooped me up and carried me to the bedroom, which was also completely white. As he laid me down, he leaned over and ever so gently placed his lips on mine. My center melted into a swirling vortex as he crawled on top of me. Then I caught myself. Was it too soon? What about protection? I was on the pill, but…"Steve, um, I'm not really ready for—"

"For me? Honey, I have been ready for you all my life."

He rolled off to my side, and propped up his head to gaze down at me. I turned on my side to face him, my hands and knees drawn up in a modified fetal position, while he had his hand on my waist, gently pulling me toward him.

"No, I just, it's just…I'm just scared."

"There is nothing to be afraid of," he breathed in my ear, "I am falling in love with you."

He looked at me in that way again. And the last remnants of any shields vanished.

6. FALLING DOWN

We were relaxing on the sofa one morning as he noticed a car pull into the driveway. A well-dressed, ordinary-looking, middle-aged brunette got out of the car and walked to the door.

"Oh my god, it's Jane." He begged me to answer the door and tell her he wasn't there as he ran downstairs to hide from her. I did what he asked, but she didn't buy it. She pushed past me into the house, stomped down the stairs to the den, and looked behind a door. And Steve started giggling. She stalked back out of the house with Steve following her with a pathetic "Wait, Jane. I'm sorry. C'mon, wait."

From the window, I watched them argue in the driveway. She soon got in her car and gunned it out to the street. He trudged back in, slumped on the sofa, and stared at the floor in stony silence. I stood across the room from him, shifting my gaze from the window to him and back again. Finally I walked over and stood in front of him.

"You slept with her, didn't you?"

"Almost."

I crossed my arms and looked down at him. "What exactly is that supposed to mean?" I kept my arms crossed.

"It's over. There's no one else. Trust me."

"How long did you see her? She seemed pretty upset."

"We dated a few months. I knew we weren't quite right, but I didn't have the heart to break it off, and she was just...incredibly persistent. I stopped calling her, but she kept calling me. The last time I saw her was a month before I met you. I'm shooting straight with you, Mandy; there really is no one else."

I let it go at that.

The next thing I knew, I was waiting for the results of my first HIV test. We had not used protection a couple of times, and he told me that he had not bothered with it much with Jane. So over the next few months, with the continued focus on AIDS in the media at that time, he had gotten edgy and said both of us needed to get tested.

Now, I knew the chances of my being positive were slim, but even that smidgen of a chance was *so* unnerving that I couldn't shake the catatonic fear. After I got tested, I just sat there, staring at the calendar, calculating my chances. If I could imagine the nurse saying the word *positive* to me, I thought it was possible. To make matters worse, Steve had told me that one of his high school classmates had AIDS. *My parents were right*, I told myself, *sex would kill me.*

Falling into the ravine between knowing and feeling was like walking between the living and the dead. I wanted to be tough. I wanted to be strong. I wanted to live my life outside a bubble. So I had to take those risks and still land on my feet. In spite of my actions to the contrary, self-sufficiency was my goal. Marriage was only a worn-out social institution, after all, like any other pointless law or custom, I told myself. And I wasn't one to fall in line with the kind of conformist thinking that carried on that ludicrous tradition.

How can we tell whether our beliefs are a result of our own independent thought and *not* a result of a civilization that kneads us into spineless masses of malleable mush? That was one of the many questions Steve and I discussed. He certainly didn't believe in marriage. He could still love me, regardless of whether or not he was even with me. But I had made the lover's leap too soon. Since he was a man and twelve years older than I was, he had a tighter grip on his emotions than I did. And this fact I despised.

Could I wash it all away and start over with the truth? I was on the verge of believing that he was not as principled or as pure a character as I was, but I couldn't even see myself as very pure anymore. He was trying to save me from himself, so I figured, if he didn't call, he was trying to be good to me. I started taping messages to myself on the phone receiver, such as, "Don't do it!" or "Stop and think!"

I should put those on the refrigerator door too.

My mere twenty-six years were merging together, washing up on the shore of my heart, wearing away my innocence like old stones. The world secretly mocked me for being a real person in an unreal world.

Oh, the HIV test came back negative. That was close.

7. SAVING LETTERS

Before the Christmas party, Steve and I went out to buy a dress, but the dress was really for him, not for me. We wound up choosing a black taffeta skirt and matching jacket, and he decided long red gloves would add some holiday flair. I was just a decoration for his ego, after all.

He told me the best thing for me was to develop my career, whatever that was. "I need assets, not liabilities," he would say. Sure. I wanted to outdistance him. But alone? There was a time when I thrived on solitude, but at that time I just felt lonely. Was he trying to tell me we didn't even have a bona fide relationship but just a friendship with a little sex thrown in? What was I making such a fuss about then? Not only would he never be affected by me, he would never admit that we even had a real relationship.

The party was near the Denver Tech Center where he worked. I had never been to any company Christmas party, and I was tremulous in that situation, to say the least. We walked in, and he began introducing me to his cohorts as his friend. This felt like a major affront to my delicate self-esteem at the time, but I tried my best to be cordial. He went about mingling, assuming that I would also be confident enough to do such a thing and would be fine on my own in a room full of strangers. Not so much. After watching him chatting with another woman, I felt queasy, and my feet found the door.

Feeling abandoned, I wandered about the hall, looking out the window at the moon and wishing I was that far away. Shortly he came looking for me, and I had to explain my neurotic behavior. We should have made things clear from the beginning as to how I would be introduced. I had to admit that I could not deal with him talking to another woman. He seemed impatient with this apparent immaturity and brushed it off. Then he more gently asked me to come back inside and told me he would use the title "girlfriend."

Later that night we again discussed the issues of marriage and commitment. We had met six months prior, and I was naturally starting to wonder "where this is going." According to his thinking, women have the "circuitry" to marry and reproduce, while men have only the circuitry to "spread the seed." He was a computer geek after all;

everything was about programming—the simulated over the real. I had to agree that there wasn't anything remotely logical about signing a lifetime contract based on something as ephemeral as a human relationship, but I was still left with the dubious open-ended question of how our story would ultimately unfold.

After finally establishing residency, I started school at the University of Colorado in January of 1991 in the teacher certification program instead of dance. I could not see what an MFA would do that a BFA would not do, except qualify me to teach dance at the college level, which I did not want to do. Teaching ballet to spoiled rich girls just didn't seem very substantial to me.

English being the other of my two greatest loves, I thought I could easily get a job teaching high school English and do the dance and writing in the summer and on weekends. My parents liked the idea, and I thought it would only take a couple of years. Teaching seemed like a solution to my income problem, and I would be helping kids, even though it would initially require a student loan of some sort. No problem, I thought. English teachers were in demand.

My parents visited Boulder that January, and Steve actually met them at the apartment. It was an awkward meeting, to say the least. That night we talked a long time in my room, and I read him a book my mother had given me when I was ten. It was a hippie edict from the seventies: *Hope for the Flowers* (Trina Paulus, 1972). He was completely blown away by this book and proclaimed that it was the story of his life—the caterpillar metamorphosis as an analogy for human growth. He didn't leave. He spent the night, saying he would leave up until about one in the morning. It was the best night we'd ever had—on a twin bed with my parents in the next room. Perhaps he would come around after all.

In the space of the next month, I sprained my ankle, Karen and I moved out to different places, and Steve informed me that he was moving to Idaho in the spring. He had the chance to live near Lake Coeur d'Alene, being burnt out from working ten years full time in the city. "It's a gift from God," he told me, "a calling I have to follow."

God. What a concept. If we just do thus and so, our spirits will live on forever in a delightful place—or perhaps move up the evolutionary ladder. The concept just never seemed revolutionary enough for a rebel like me.

I wrote volumes of soul-searching letters to Steve after he moved, sitting at my tiny desk facing a wall, with my mattress back on the floor, in a closet-like room in a house on Bluff Street. He finally responded after what seemed like a quarter of a century.

He again laid out all his reasons why he thought marriage or even living together was a bad idea in general, and he went on and on about figuring out his purpose in life. In his mind, there was something beyond marriage and parenting that was far more important, but he never delineated it, except by referring to angels and their priorities. He supported my creative endeavors, galvanized me to leave my parents in my dust, and begged me to stop worrying about the future, since worrying doesn't change a thing. And there was love—or at least a well-worded statement to that effect. At the very end there was a request: he asked me not to save his letters. I did, of course, but they are starting to disintegrate.

8. ALTITUDE

Steve came back for a visit in July, so finally we went hiking together. Rebelling against my feminist instinct that kept telling me I did not have to look good just for a man, I had dieted and exercised strenuously in preparation for his visit. And he demonstrated his approval. I had to try to make him sorry he left. We bought a few overpriced items at the health-food store and headed off for the foothills.

At last I was leading the way—a novel experience for Steve. Having hiked the Royal Arch trail many times before, I knew every incline and switchback. But it always seemed endless, snaking its way over jagged boulders and around tree roots, finally arriving at a rocky overlook, only to descend downward and straight back up again.

Steve trailed behind me, not at all happy with his position. I enjoyed being the leader so much that I forgot how irritated and hurt I had been about the fact that he had not come to Boulder specifically to visit me, but was actually on his way to take care of some "personal business" in Texas.

"Where are you going?" His exasperation entertained me as I charged up the relentless trail, but his question was directed more toward the trail than toward me. When we finally reached the apex and took in the view, he forgot how arduous the hike had been. We relaxed on the flat rock and gazed out over Denver. The brown cloud could not be overlooked. "This area is poisonous," he said. "That right there is half the reason I moved to Idaho. You'll love it up there, Mandy. Wait till you see it."

"I know. I know. Idaho has to be more pristine than this, but you take the good with the bad. I love Boulder—walking out the door and being up here in a matter of minutes without having to drive. And Boulder is cleaner than Denver; we bike here."

The conversation waned, and we were silent.

He broke the silence. "This is Lucifer's world, you know."

I would have laughed if he hadn't spoken with such dead seriousness. "What do you mean? If this world is messed up, it's man's fault."

"That's because Lucifer is so influential down here. Don't you remember? Lucifer was cast out of heaven and he fell to Earth. I want out of this place. The only way to get out is to grow beyond it. The world is like school, Mandy. You have to learn your lessons so you can graduate."

He stated all of this with such conviction that I felt compelled to agree. I absorbed it and was silent, but it was hard to think of the Earth as hell. It endured so much mistreatment, and yet it kept on giving. We relaxed side by side in the sun for a long time.

In August, I nabbed a ride to Idaho. At almost twenty-seven, I still didn't own a car, so I consulted the Ride Board on campus and found a woman who was going my way. The trip was an adventure in itself, being my first road trip since I had moved to Colorado. Heading off into the great wide open, we sped along in her Saab across the high plains of Wyoming and Montana. I was hooked for life.

As we crested the Bitterroot Mountain Range, the views became more breathtaking. Huge swaths of pine trees ascended on both sides of the highway. Then there were the lakes—Lake Coeur d'Alene in particular. The expanse of sparkling blue water against the backdrop of still more timberland and mountains in the distance was a view of heaven itself.

The road wound its way into the small town, and we found his house in a wooded neighborhood, hidden from view from the road by tall pines. The butterflies were jumping (in my stomach) as we pulled into his driveway.

All my anger had dissipated during the trip, and after hugging, he showed me around the house. There was a huge deck with a hot tub and a backyard that merged with the woods. He had started dinner and seemed genuinely glad to see me. The place felt like home almost immediately.

The first few days were like a vacation for me, but the tension remained between us, as so many issues were left unresolved. He said he wanted to be celibate for a time as a way to clear his head, but this was difficult for me to accept, as we had always had a great physical aspect to our relationship.

We took his brother's motorboat out for a jaunt up the waterway that emptied into the lake. Then we stopped at a small cafe that perched on an inlet along the lakeshore. They were famous there for a drink called the Derailer, having something to do with the logging industry. We were drowsy under the stars on the way back, and he made an exception to his celibacy rule that night.

9. REVELATIONS

Sitting at the kitchen counter the next morning, he said he had something he wanted me to look at and brought in a box of papers from the garage. He sorted through the materials; some of them looked like government documents. Then he handed me a folder. "Just take a look at this and tell me what you think."

The articles all dealt with cattle mutilations, conjectures about aliens, and government cover-ups. "Is this the kind of stuff that's in *all* those boxes out there?" I asked.

"This and a lot of government information that not many people know about. The government hides so much from us, Mandy. You would be astounded if you knew the truth."

He watched me closely as I tentatively perused the articles, which seemed like tabloid material. "What do you think did this?" he asked, referring to the mutilations.

"Probably someone looking for fifteen minutes of fame at the expense of a bull. What's this all about anyway?"

"Back in 1975, I was friends with someone who knew a lot about it, and he opened my eyes in a way that changed my life. I just want you to look at these articles carefully, and then I have some other things I think you should read."

He was inscrutable. Masses of material were expunged from his garage over the next few days.

One night he casually mentioned the fact that he had another friend named Sheila, from work in Denver, and he was thinking of inviting her for a visit. He asked if I'd be OK with that, assuring me that there was no romantic interest between them.

I thought nothing of it. I did not reveal to him that I had actually slept with a gorgeous twenty-two-year-old in late July. When I say "slept," I mean just that; there was no sex. So since I hadn't actually had intercourse with the guy, I did not view it as a betrayal. Why cause a problem by mentioning it?

It was near the end of our time together when we were holding each other in the hot tub. "I've longed for this ever since you left," I breathed.

"Then think about moving up here. We could work together on some projects I have going. I can write music, and you can sing."

"But I just started school in Boulder, and you don't want a long-term commitment."

"Maybe you don't need to go to school right now. There are so many other things you could be doing."

"Sure there are, but do they make money?"

"You worry about money too much. Sometimes if you just trust, everything you need comes to you. You just have to keep moving forward and sending out positive vibrations."

We were silent for a moment. Then my mind wandered back to the old off-limits topic. "Steve, do you really think you won't marry again?"

His eyes lost their lively glint, as he was clearly tired of having to address the subject. "Mandy—no, I just can't see myself doing that again. Why do you persist in thinking that we need that kind of legal trap to call our relationship legitimate? I love you and want to share part of my life with you, but I just need this solitude right now. I need you to understand that."

I crawled out of that cauldron, went inside, sat down in the hallway, and cried.

To try to make things better and to enable me to visit him on my own, he found me a rusty, brown 1970 Chevy Nova. The gears were loose and it had rear-wheel drive, but I could finally travel in style, as in, with my own wheels.

The house on Bluff Street sold by the end of the summer, so I found my fourth makeshift rental situation, this time on Thirty-First near an entrance to the bike path. My roommate was a forty-six-year-old woman into rebirthing and food combining, and she was the most anal woman I had ever known. She loved my car. Just kidding.

I took "The Bible as Literature," *and* "Women Writers" at the same time that fall. A heavy course load helped me to concentrate on something else. For a few months at least.

But Steve managed to visit one night near the end of September. He brought wine. The next morning, I told him I had met a man in July, but I swore that I had not had sex with him. Steve was silent for a moment. Then he told me that he too had a confession. He took a deep breath. "Sheila is more than just a friend; I was with her last night."

My teeth clenched. *Last night?*

He continued. "Well, you know, it's been a long time for me, and she started coming on really strong. I woke up thinking of you. I feel like I've betrayed you."

Staring straight through him, I replied, "You have."

I rolled off the mattress and bolted from the room to avoid just lying there, letting the words sink in, and allowing the tears to trickle down the sides of my head. Besides, I had my high- powered aerobics job to go to that morning. This revelation was not what I wanted to hear that morning—or ever. After all, up until then I had only heard the mention of her name once, in passing. Perhaps I should have expected it, but I was living in a dream bubble that prevented me from even considering such a possibility.

I cried in the shower.

When I came back into the room, he was sitting at my desk, scribbling down some list. He was always making lists. I was dressed to teach class, and when he saw me, he pulled me to him and pressed his head against my belly. "Oh my god, you are gorgeous. How could I have been with Sheila when I could've been with this?"

"I have no idea." I smiled coldly at him.

Before he left, he made a vow of celibacy. He swore he would not have sex with either of us.

In his next letter, he mentioned matters of conscience in dealing with the flesh and spirit. It seemed like he wanted us to be even closer than we had been, in spite of "the insane addictions of this world." And then he asked me to consider moving up there, while reiterating his stance on celibacy. This was a confounding situation, and my whole world began to feel surreal, like I was trapped in that Jackson Pollack painting while the paint was being thrown. Inexplicably I still loved him and *wanted* him, more and more. But there was always a roadblock.

10. WAR GAMES

During Thanksgiving break, which I spent alone, I called him one night and found out that not only was Sheila there, but that he had told her he loved her. It finally dawned on me that there was far more to this affair than I had been led to believe. She would go up there again, there was no doubt, and I could not cope with the thought of that. There was no one else in my life except him, which was dangerous, since he was trying to take over my mind.

He acted like he knew how I should think and feel better than I knew. He was constantly evaluating me in some way: how I looked, how little money I had, how I conducted myself, how well I did or didn't clean up after myself, ad nauseam. He had a set of standards in mind that I had to meet or beat. And all this while his own actions continued to contradict his words.

For someone who hadn't really had a "relationship" for the past five years, he was leaving an awfully long trail of broken hearts. I was getting burned again, so I had to take my hand off the burner. Only a masochist loves someone who hurts her. Time heals all wounds, but it can't replace an amputated leg. Some wounds are just too deep.

I was just a human being, a life form that wasn't good enough to have a bond with him. He added a new dimension to egotism. What was I losing anyway? I would not be a doll he took out of his drawer to play with four times a year.

There was one last trek to Idaho in January of 1992 to try to tie up loose ends. I busted my ass to make it there before night fell and ice formed on the road. We decided to rent a video the night I arrived. As we pulled into the Blockbuster parking lot, I broached the subject of *her.* I asked if my confession about the young guy in July was the reason he had become closer to Sheila.

"No, Mandy, that's not it. That has nothing to do with it."

"It doesn't? But I don't understand then. Why?"

He sighed heavily, stared straight ahead at the lights in the store, and machine gunned his next phrase: "Because-I-was-with-Sheila-before-you-were-with-him. Now let's go." He got out of the car as if it were about to explode.

My mouth fell open. *Before?*

I stared at him as he walked around the front of the car as if he was actually going into the store. He looked at me, came over to my side of the car, and opened the door. He knelt down and put his head on my knee while gathering the courage to meet my gaze. When he finally looked up at me, there was nothing recognizable in those eyes of steel. He put his head back in my lap.

I spoke first. “I don’t know you.”

(Silence.)

“I’m leaving.”

“Now, come on, don’t leave,” he whined.

“Give me one good reason not to.”

“Because I love you.”

“I’m supposed to believe you now?”

“I haven’t lied to you. I just didn’t tell you about Sheila. The fact that I love you has never been a lie.”

“Love means honesty and commitment. I have never received either of those from you.”

“I know, and you’ve got to help me with that. I love you for your honesty, because that’s something I have a problem with. I’m untrustworthy in relationships. Can you forgive me?”

My head was swimming. *Forgive him?* He hadn’t even said he was sorry yet. I hadn’t even begun to survey the damage. But as I stared out the window at the stars on the way home, struggling to see the light, I regained the presence of mind to realize I had to dig for the whole story.

When we got back to the house, I convinced him to call Sheila so that I could question her directly to get to the bottom of the whole sordid affair. He warned me that she would probably exaggerate certain episodes for the purpose of twisting the knife in deeper. I told him I didn’t care. He obviously thought I was a fragile glass doll who had to be shielded from the shattering truth.

He called her. "Yeah, I told her. She knows, but she wants to talk to you."

I took the phone from him. "Sheila?"

"Hello. Are you OK? I can't believe he hid this from you for so long. I told him to tell you. What did he tell you exactly?"

"He...just said that you two were together before I met this other guy in July. But nothing happened, I was just being honest. But I thought that was the reason he decided to keep seeing you."

"Honey, we met way back in March."

"*March?!*" Episodes flashed through my head. "But y—you were just—friends, right?"

"Hardly. We were very physical from the moment we met. We had sex all the time—every time we saw each other. I helped him move up there, and we had sex on the floor as soon as we got into the house."

I froze inside and stared wide-eyed at Steve. His face was contorted with guilt.

"You were here—first?"

"Oh yeah, I've been up there lots of times since he moved. Look, I love Steve and—"

"Oh, and you think I don't? Listen, we've been involved since July of 1990. I thought he wanted solitude, so I didn't force myself on him after he moved."

"July of 1990? He told me he wasn't involved with anyone when we met."

"He obviously lied. We had a few problems, but we resolved them. We never actually broke up."

"Well, I took time off work to be with him. He wanted me there from what I could tell. I was up there in July for over a week and September for a weekend and ten days in October and then Thanksgiving, but at least you know about that."

I was unraveling fast. My voice quivered. "He told me he had sex with you for the first time in September," I breathed, "and then he vowed celibacy."

"Yes, he did make that vow, and I think he's upheld it, but we were very active up until September."

"You didn't have sex in October?"

"To be honest, I really can't remember. I know we weren't as physical as we were in July. God, we had sex all the time then, every room, especially in the hot tub—at least six or seven times in there."

A cannon ball ripped through my chest. I dropped the phone and ran screaming into the bedroom. As I writhed in utter anguish on the bed, I imagined that they had sex on that bed as well. My mind was drawn to its own destruction.

11. ON THE VERGE

I realized then that salvation could never be found in another human being, so I immediately set to work on becoming my own salvation. What was it that kept me from succumbing to utter despair?

All my mind could do was conjure up images of them making love on the floor, in the hot tub, even in her apartment. But all that didn't seem to make any difference in how he actually felt about her or me. Not having sex did not diminish the emotional connection between us. By the same token, after a certain point, sex did nothing to deepen any emotional connection either. "Love Is Blindness" by U2 was my dark song of choice that matched my mood all the way home. I truly did not want to see, but I was being forced to see.

When I got home, I felt like I was walking into a stranger's room. The person who lived there before 1992 no longer existed. I cleared out my closet, throwing out the remnants of adolescence and innocence. Long-term monogamy, I decided, was utterly unattainable. I'd already been intimate with ten men by that point. What did that mean? Did it matter? No one can escape their sexuality. We are all either male or female; we can't get out of our bodies as long as we are humans on this Earth.

Despite the three-way blowout on the phone, I found I could actually talk to Sheila after I got back, and thus we began to throw back the cloak of deceit that Steve was hiding behind. Books were shoved off the desk and school became a sideline activity. Of course, she didn't know any of the truth about me. We compared notes in a way that was in *our* best interests.

How could I be suspicious of him and still love him? Love is a mysterious thing. Every little thing he said could be a clue, the tip of another iceberg. Something was on the verge of discovery every moment. Was that what I was looking for? Something to write about? A roller-coaster ride just so I could feel alive?

It was as if he had both a wife and a mother. Maybe that's why many men remain single. Steve did not seem to be the kind of man who would tolerate having two women constantly checking up on him for very long. I remembered him looking drawn and taut all through the month of May, but it wasn't the impending move that was the major stressor, it was his guilt.

I had to sift through all of the past year piece by piece, deducing his motives at every turn. In order to see through him, I became obsessed with the dynamics of his deceit.

Sheila and I became sisters of a sort, having the common goal of wanting to punish this man for being so deceitful to both of us. Being women, we could understand each other's pain, but at least we had some degree of power. We could also see the quandary that Steve was in. He had been booted out of the cardboard Eden his lies had built.

Yet she was still determined to move up there, which was astounding to me, but I could do nothing to dissuade her. Familiarity would breed contempt, I told myself, plus she would have to get lost while I was visiting.

Then it hit me: all this was because the universe was pulling me back to my senses, back to my real objectives in life. Thoughts of traveling, of rising above, of getting beyond, pulled me up and away from the quagmire. Steve was just a boy learning the lessons he should have learned long ago.

A few weeks later, he called to tell me about a videotape he had received from a group of friends in California. He told me it was about the Second Coming and that the person speaking on the tape was from the Kingdom of God. He had sent it to me and to Sheila, as well as two friends in Denver. The group was called Total Overcomers Anonymous. He "revealed" to me on the phone that he was an alien, not of this world. Go figure. Perhaps the tapes would show me the method of Steve's madness.

After the first five minutes of watching the video, I thought, *So this is why Steve is so sick; he's been in a cult for thirteen years!* But I continued listening anyway to the wide-eyed, shaved-head, sixty-plus-year-old man as he lectured intently about humanness, angels, heaven, and awakenings. Somehow the guy just didn't sound like he was preaching. He kept repeating the word "humanness" with disdain, like it was a disease. I wanted him to define his terms. *Perhaps the trauma of Steve's deceit was my awakening*, I thought. What is there to *do* in heaven? What do angels think about? Could I still go hiking if I joined this group? The body was just a vehicle of expression according to this new thinking. Tests in life were supposed to lead to growth toward God.

Sheila and I continued our phone conversations, only now it was almost as if we were competing in how fast we could be converted, in how spiritual we were. I always rise to meet a challenge, so I entered into this spiritual duel. After all, we started out as competitors for the same man; this just raised the stakes.

The cult members made it clear that the choice to follow them should not be based on our feelings for Steve. So the question was, who would be able to prove that she was both spiritually "fit" *and* no longer emotionally attached to Steve, in order to be "invited" into the monastery? We had to vie for election to be part of this elite group.

My mind started grasping for distractions from the pain and confusion, yet I also felt a rising anticipation. This new information opened up a whole new collection of questions: How many times had he changed his name? Would he change it again? Jesus's disciples did not own a Buick Riviera with a stellar sound system. Would he be easily forgiven for the sex, deceit, and materialism?

Wouldn't they make him atone for his sins? The reason I was so drawn to Steve had to have something to do with his involvement in this group. At least, that's how it seemed at the time.

So much of my life suddenly seemed to make sense. First everything fell apart with the discovery of Steve's deceit, then the pieces started coming together and forming a whole new picture. Was this really *it?* And all that time I had thought it was a crazy dream of mine: the longing to get free of this place and time, to escape from myself, to get out of this body—but not by dying physically.

I was at once both fearful and joyous. Why had I come in contact with that information at that particular time? Why were the words of Jesus suddenly speaking straight to my heart and making more sense than ever? I decided that *God* was indeed teaching me the final lessons I needed to learn in order to graduate to His House. It explained why I had always felt alienated from my family and society. It explained why I was so drawn to teach and create. It explained why I had to struggle with gender and sex.

It explained why I was so determined to keep my body clean, lean, and strong. It explained why I had never aimed for money nor understood any focus on the material world. All the dating mess suddenly seemed like utter nonsense. There was no way I'd ever take up the search for Mr. Right again.

12. PUZZLE

Every aspect of my academic life seemed associated with this new Tower of Babble, from the "Bible as Literature" to *The Canterbury Tales* to Wollstonecraft as she advocated a more genderless society. I figured that if I had already devoted my life to such intangibles as creativity and expression, if I had always felt that this planet was only one of many, and if I had always believed that humans have unlimited potential to grow beyond themselves—then believing that a representative of God was on this Earth in a human form didn't seem like such a stretch. The group truly believed they were bringing the same message as Jesus did.

They originally took on the name Human Individual Metamorphosis. They changed the name again to keep things fresh and to try to capture the essence of what they were about. It was about "dropping all behavior not common to Heaven": old attachments, ties that bind, addictions—generally all habits common to humans. Jesus had told his disciples to drop everything and follow him and to overcome the world, after all.

The group had written a statement and spent nine months traveling around the country in the early seventies. They started with a hundred students, but the numbers quickly dropped off to around twenty. They had to keep moving, since a lot of people were not pleased with what they had to say. I wondered what the guy did before he started his clan. What would make someone become so obsessed with a cockeyed mission like that?

They said it took a gift from Heaven to get you with their representative, and when you got the gift, nothing else would mean anything anymore. Jesus was just one representative, and it wasn't about just accepting Jesus: you had to become *like* Jesus, and that was a tough act to follow. "You may feel like everything is falling apart when you are going through your awakening," the leader preached. How, specifically? Overcoming gender consciousness was another major point of theirs, and it hit home with me. What's the *point* of being conscious of gender anyway? How freeing to stop remembering that I'm a girl!

The human world, they said, was designed not to work. God would take stuff away as you asked Him to, but would leave the hard stuff to make you strong. The hard stuff was the human need for physical affection, attention, and the ego. You had to give up *Self*.

It seemed like a return to innocence, a reaffirmation of a faith that had been submerged underneath layers of crass cynicism. God was giving me the courage to scrape away these layers and get back to my core. What had weighed me down suddenly lifted me up. What had blocked my way was propelling me forward. What had confused me was bringing clarity.

Being entirely distracted from school, I walked into the registrar's office and told the lady I was joining a monastery and needed to withdraw. She raised her eyebrows and then gave me the paperwork without question. After I walked out of the office, I commenced with my election campaign.

Feb. 11, 1992

Dear TOA:

I have been exposed to the first two videos through one of your students. This particular person has caused a great deal of recent change in my life.

In July of 1990, I met Steve through a personal ad. We meshed well immediately, but then an issue with trust emerged, and he maintained that he did have a problem with honesty. He told me he loved me mainly because I was so honest.

But Steve carried on with both me and another woman, keeping us both oblivious, for almost a year. When he finally spilled it, I insisted on a rather devastating three-way phone conversation. It is this traumatic experience that I call my "awakening." I was hurt so deeply that I will never be the same. Yet if it hadn't happened, I would not have this chance to grow.

It all showed me that God clearly does not want me to have a human relationship with a man and I was forced to look to God for strength. It opened up my heart and mind to new ways of relating to people, not to men and women. The idea of a genderless society is quite appealing to me. Society, not God, made me a "woman." Sex has always baffled me. I want to forget I'm a woman and be relieved of all the pressures that go along with being a woman in this world.

This world has always seemed a foreign place to me and I have always felt like an outsider. I was the rebel in my family and moved away when I was 18. I have always believed that this life is neither my first nor my last. "Human Individual Metamorphosis" is a concept with which I can connect because I experience fleeting transformations when I dance.

Now I know what Steve meant all this time when he used the phrase "beyond human." I thought he was advocating that humans become more like computers, without needs or emotions. Now I know he was talking about overcoming our human weaknesses so that we can enter the Kingdom of God. Yet—I wonder how he could have committed so many transgressions after having done so much work to become "pure."

I have never been materialistic in any way. I've never accepted the world as it is, but have focused instead on how it could be. I've always felt I have some special purpose in my life and that God has helped me and shown me the way. I have always known that I was not born to fit into this society as it stands, but to change it by changing my own heart as well as reaching out to other hearts. I'm always trying to become clearer, more receptive, purer in my motives, and more energetic in moving in the direction God shows me.

My ego may be hardest to overcome since I am an initiator and not a follower. It is very hard for me to listen to anyone and swallow every word.

Hope this is not too overwhelming—

Mandy

13. LOADED

The next day I drove to Sheila's apartment to help her move. This was to be the first and only time we would ever meet, and I thought I was incredibly mature to be able to do this. We both knew Steve would return to the cult by the end of February, so the threat of her winning the battle for him was defused. He was pulling away, which was a relief valve for all of us.

When Sheila and I met, I didn't feel as threatened by her as I thought I would. *This* was the woman who caused me so much agony? She wasn't cute or voluptuous or striking in any way. But it felt eerie to look around her apartment knowing that Steve had been there—often.

We loaded the little trailer she had hitched onto the back of her Golf hatchback, which I doubted had enough horsepower to tote the load over the mountains. I looked out over the Rockies every time I mounted the stairs. Where would I go next? But I couldn't dwell on that for long; I was training myself not to be so self-centered, since I too was considering entering the cult.

They wrote to me again and sent me more videos. Steve told me to watch the tapes two or three times, because they were "very potent."

It made sense to me: the Earth was completely covered and explored, so next would come the outer realm. It seemed logical to believe that the Human Kingdom was simply another rung on the evolutionary ladder, but why should we think that the Human Kingdom is as high as we go? Nature recycles itself, and so must human souls. Humans didn't create original human life; the world can't be arbitrary, because nature has a pattern. And Jesus wasn't crucified because he followed the herd.

I didn't have to destroy everything; I just had to leave it behind, break all the ties—almost like what I tried to do by leaving Michigan. I figured I'd just put everything into storage and have my family come and get it eventually. How could I have explained?

The group didn't ask for money. They weren't really persuading anyone to attempt this changeover. It wasn't supposed to be some kind of cop-out trip. They wanted people to become more kind, not less, so they told us not to leave a mess when we made our exit, but rather to use discretion. They didn't want us leaving others with the impression that we had flipped out.

That part would be tough.

We were talking about the Second Coming, after all. Was seeing my mother again more important than that? Was producing another show more important? Was teaching high school more important? *No! The world was about to be recycled!* That's why Steve never recycled.

As I continued watching the videos, the wide-eyed, bald man drew a picture of the universe that was a surreal diversion from any vision I had ever conjured up. He also delineated specific behavior expectations I could look forward to if I were inducted into the group. I would have to do tasks that might not develop my specific talents, eat whatever was available, and cut my hair. I would have to be a servant available to work, to make a contribution. There was to be no competitive nature, no need to feel special among others. That would be very difficult for my egotistical self.

I would have to become literally unable to remember the past, because it was dangerous to even reflect. There was to be no questioning, only trust, always looking to the Next Level. Negativity was a limit. There was to be no hiding. You had to overcome embarrassment. Things were not predetermined; it was all step by step. You had to remain adaptable. No labels were allowed; labels were a limit. There were no comparisons to be made. Energy should go vertically, not laterally, he taught.

You could hold nothing for yourself, losing your Self entirely. He mentioned experiencing "birth pangs" that would occur throughout the process that would be unlike anything I had ever experienced. The soul would come to life as the flesh died. The group was not concerned with the death of the vehicle (body), only the death of the soul.

There was an emphasis on speeding up the process, as there was only a limited time in which to complete this transition. Structure was paramount; after all, this was preparation for God's astronaut program. Sin was anything you did that separated you from God. Death was when the mind of God in your soul had shrunk so much that your soul was not redeemable.

I pulled back for a bit to try to get a little breathing room.

I asked them if perhaps I could just spend some time with them to see what they were all about, sort of an internship of sorts. But no, you had to be invited into their Household. It had to be all you wanted, and there could be no other options in your mind. They reminded me that leaving my life behind and attempting this transition based only my feelings for Steve would be unwise. They quoted the Book of Matthew as they explained the celibacy stance. I asked about daily activities, and they informed me that they had "mundane" domestic chores to do and that they kept up with current events as they were so indicative of the "End of the Age."

A week later, Steve's sister, Diana, called me around eleven at night and told me "they" wanted to meet with us in a hotel in Denver. We drove separately to the hotel near the Tech Center and were escorted to a conference room on the top floor. A short-haired, gender-neutral duo proceeded to grill us to try to ascertain if we were interested in the group solely because of Steve. Of course, we were, but we managed to convince them otherwise. Their purpose in the visit was to make us sweat and to show us that these people actually existed in the flesh. As we left the hotel, we hugged each other and looked up at the moon with a twinkle in our eyes, as if we had some secret knowledge.

"I feel so—special," I said.

"You are," she answered.

You had to go through hell to get to heaven, but anything you used as a crutch to get you through hell would keep you in hell. According to them, the world was designed in such a way as to make weaker souls have a need for many crutches to keep them here longer. Souls only got stronger by going through many lives and lessons over the past age. For those who fell into the trap of worshipping the world and their lives here, life would be nothing but frustration and disappointment. Yet those were necessary lessons they had to learn before they too could finally awaken. The world was simply a place to grow *up*.

To have guidance! To have a mentor! To have a chance to be part of "God's crew"! To be given a point of reference that enabled me to block out so much static. It was total liberation, a total rebirth. Nothing could have been more appealing, because I was so tired of my old mindset, the old vicious circles. I always knew that everything would come to a dead end sooner or later, because salvation could never be found on Earth.

None of this would have felt so true to me if it hadn't already been in my soul, I told myself. To others, it was just something to find fault with or it was simply beyond their comprehension. It was too much for them to take; they didn't have the faith to believe that a real representative from the Kingdom of Heaven could actually be on Earth in a human form. I had never heard of anyone claiming this, and who in their right mind would? Why would he put himself through that? *No one* would attempt such an undertaking unless he had truly undergone some monumental shift. The group knowingly subjected itself to scorn and ridicule. There must have been some intense urgency driving them forward in spite of everything.

If I wound up with them and felt that the group was my *true* family, I wouldn't ever want to leave them. But what if I saw Steve again? Part of the reason I was stubborn about not pulling out was that I knew Sheila might get in. And I was sure she was thinking the same thing. So on we went with the competition; nothing would be over just because Steve went back to the cult. I had to reprogram myself not to care about that. I had to learn not to love him.

After said years with *no* sex or physicality, what would you expect? Was he really ready to break with his humanness? I decided I just had to meet these people, meet the leader, find out how they really lived, and see what these "tasks" and "experiments" really were. That way I could decide if it really was for me. I loved every aspect of it, *except* the loss of independence.

I wanted to see if I could "make it" and witness Steve in a more refined state. But if he couldn't maintain that state in the outside world, had he really overcome anything?

Perhaps the group was a bit *too* exclusive and reclusive. They thought that since they were preparing to leave this world anyway, why deal with it? I had to agree with their premise that the End of the Age was fast approaching in order to rationalize their practice of seclusion. Otherwise the monastery could only be viewed as a retreat of sorts—and for Steve, that's what it had been, for thirteen years.

Signs of the End Times have always been apparent, because time has no beginning and no end. So the End of the Age premise was becoming a bit shaky in my mind. Could I believe that I had actually been given the key to Heaven, that I was one of "the chosen"? Getting free of the world was one thing, but getting free of myself was another.

14. BLACK HOLE

"In order to find yourself, you must lose yourself."
St. Francis of Assisi

I finally had to admit that there was no guarantee that anything this guy said was actually coming from God. Furthermore, the Bible has been through hundreds of translations and revisions and wasn't even firsthand to begin with. Everything was a matter of pure faith. I gathered the courage to speak my mind to them, knowing they would not like my statements.

Dear TOA:

Some other concerns broke through to me today. Since I know that I am not the source of my messages—perhaps I can also say that I too am a representative from the Kingdom of Heaven. Perhaps there are other representatives—lots of others—because God can utilize endless avenues. I know this because I can see the diversity of the human garden and in the plant and animal kingdoms as well. I hope I am not being irreverent to suggest such a thing, but it entered my mind and I want to be open with you.

How can one say they have "overcome the world" when they are in seclusion from it? It seems to me that the true measure of how much we have overcome can only be gauged by how well we can maintain our principles while IN the world, NOT while we are under the protection of a controlled group in a controlled environment. We all know it's easier to be studious while in school than it is after we leave the academic haven, and easier to stay on a diet while at a health spa than at home in our kitchen. So the question is ultimately: Can we uphold said principles without using the "crutch" of isolation? If 13 years didn't change Steve, how many more will it take? Or does he only need to be forgiven rather than reformed? I have to judge the tree by its fruit.

Speaking to some theologists and ministers has meant being subjected to very difficult tests. But I am not afraid. I want to be open. I want to be sure. I believe in much of what you're about and I like telling others about your principles. I still, however, don't understand the distinction you make between "free will" and "independent thinking." If I'm always free to leave you, I must think independently in order to make that decision. Yet you are telling me that I must give up independent thinking in order to follow you.

In spite of all my questions, I'm still intent on following you. I cannot turn away from this information.

Sincerely,

Mandy

I had to meet the leader. What about his free will? He seemed to want to play "follow the leader," but I wouldn't play that game. They kept telling me I didn't know and that only they had the truth. How could I recognize God in anyone but myself? Didn't I have a right to my own mind? I had to prove myself to them, but they were absolved from having to prove anything. *Anyone* can believe that their thoughts are coming from God. He said that owning anything would separate us from God, but somehow it was OK for him to own our minds.

On the night of March 17th, my phone rang. It was one of them.

"Mandy, your last letter told us that you are just not ready to graduate. I was told to call you as soon as possible."

My blood sunk to the floorboards. "Not ready? But I, but I…"

"It's best if we don't prolong this call. You just go on with your life."

"But wait," I bawled. "I'll never see Steve again, will I?"

"No, you won't."

"Can I at least write to him—through you?"

"You know we don't allow any contact with the outside world. Now I have to hang up. You just go on with your life." And she hung up. I collapsed on my mattress on the floor, and dissolved into tears.

With the way I had been thinking about the whole thing by then, you might think I wouldn't have been too upset by this rejection. But this...this was the bitter end of the relationship I was willing to go to the edge for. Never again would I hear Steve's voice, look into his eyes, or touch his hand. Yes, I only wanted to get in to stay close to him. I wanted to believe what he believed.

Love can be fatal.

Looking back, this truly was all for the best, as an invitation from them could have easily meant my death, and my parents would have been watching me give *my* "farewell speech" on the evening news. On the other hand, I never felt the same depth of love for any other man after him. It will always be a mystery to me.

15. CANYONS AND CLIFFS

The whole episode made me suspicious of everything that tried to sway me, whether religion, politics, the media, or especially corporate America. Over time, I came to believe that organized religion was just organized cultism. Everyone was just trying to institutionalize their truth and sell it as the only truth. If we think there's some sort of hierarchy in another realm that we can't get to except by being elected, then religion is just politics, and churches are nothing more than frat houses and sororities. Thank God I never joined one of *those*.

It's easy for someone to believe something if *not* believing it would alienate them from someone they love. So an emotional attachment to someone in any group almost *necessitates* joining up. It's not so much "truth," it's what *feels* like the truth or what we *want* to feel is the truth.

The media is the cult of mind control in the service of the god of commerce. The government houses a vast array of groupthink cults. Every school, every society, is a cult. We are cults unto ourselves in trying to control our own behavior, expression, and presentation, according to standards we have been conditioned to uphold. We practice self-censorship every day. Erich Fromm once wrote that the most powerful motive for self-repression is the fear of isolation. No one who fears isolation can think freely.

You can lead a person to a mirror, but you can't make him see his reflection. We can't even see our own reflection clearly when our perception is so skewed by what we have been taught to want to see.

There was simply no possible way to know the truth, but I still couldn't help but search for it. I had to be OK with just leaving it all behind without any closure. I hoped I would not be haunted by it for the rest of my life.

After watching *Thelma and Louise*, I decided I had to make another overland trek in the old Chevy Nova—this time to the Grand Canyon. I had pulled myself out of the quicksand right before I got sucked under, and I wanted to run like hell to get as far away as possible from the mudslide.

But the trip couldn't heal me in a week. It would take years. The caverns near the Grand Canyon seemed like the caverns of my heart. My spirit had endured a lot. And I felt that the Earth had way more character than any human who ever lived.

Speaking of character, I got stopped by a cop in Arizona. He apologized when he saw a white, brunette college girl driving. He explained that I just happened to be traversing a drug route and driving the type of car most often used for smuggling drugs from Mexico. Then he let me go my merry way. I was definitely moving up in the world.

On the way back to Colorado, I drove to the Mesa Verde cliffs. I had slept in the car not far from there, and the sun woke me at dawn. There was no one at the site, and I reverently proceeded up the road to the ruins. It was one of those moments I knew would never come again, even on a return visit. The early light brought out colors that illuminated parts of my brain that had never been awake, and the air made the colors vibrate.

On the way back down the road, I noticed a small boulder in my path and estimated that I would clear it, so I drove over it instead of around it. It stopped my car with a horrible screech. Only through an extended nerve-racking process of backing up and going forward did I finally wrench my lowrider off the rock.

The comfort of certainty is an illusion frequently sought after and found in all the wrong places. Answers are usually in the form of questions, because all our answers are not the answer. The universe moves at the speed of light, but the light breaks through to us only as often as we gaze at the stars. I have no answers, but I do believe in awakenings; they come when we have fallen asleep. They make us realize it's getting late, and that our lives are just sandcastles on the beach of the greater scheme of things.

Can anyone truly transcend the influences of society? What dictates the impulses of any individual? Does our compass show true north? Or does our sense of direction change with every breath we take? Are we ever the sole proprietors of our own minds? If, in the words of Rumi, we are "knocking from the inside," then we are already everywhere we want to be. But where is that?

The truth shall set us free. Under which stone shall we look for the truth? And what does it mean to be free? Free from what? To do what? What if the truth really is so "inconvenient" that none of us wants to face it? Ah well, I am, therefore I think. Life has to be examined to make it worth living, right?

16. "NEXT"

After recovering on the farm for a few months, I got back in the saddle and galloped back to Boulder, still driving the Chevy Nova. I had found renewed vigor—and renewed desire for another man. I found a room in a house near Table Mesa, this time with a couple of guys: pot-smoking chefs. But they only smoked in the den, and I was on the ground floor and finally had my own bathroom. It was worth it. But I still didn't know how to meet decent men.

I figured I'd place another personal ad and just screen more carefully. Trying to get back on my professional track, I resumed my academic trajectory, still having at least three semesters of work ahead of me before becoming certified to teach—or becoming certifiable, whichever came first.

By then I knew all too well that giving in to my instinctual desires carried a high price. But my sex drive was revving higher than ever, and I didn't know how to rein it in. I had to face the fact that there was a part of me that was so wild, so untamed, so beyond the reach of my rational mind that it beckoned me into the depths of hell. There has to be a spark before there can be a flame, but a flame can turn into a raging inferno and destroy everything in its path.

I hated leaving Mike after the first date. He was short, barely my height, and with a decidedly nasal voice, but had cute brown eyes and a full head of hair at thirty-eight. He worked in the medical field in human resources. Nothing says "marriage material" like a suit. Over lunch in Denver, he told me about what happened with his ex-fiancée. She had left him for another man, whom he said he almost killed. So he'd been in anger therapy for a few years. Great.

Could I trust him? Could I believe a word he said? Perhaps he was a murderer or a rapist—or worse, a manipulator, like some others I had known. He said he had a tendency to be controlling in a relationship, and he even had mannerisms and personality traits that reminded me of Steve. Maybe that was because Steve had not faded sufficiently from memory.

Nothing could have been worse than what happened with Steve, so I figured I could survive anything. I had resurrected my life, but I knew I had to keep my wits about me, in spite of Mike's bedroom whispers echoing through my brain. He was oozing nonsense about my living with him, him being inside me every night, him being afraid to offer his whole heart until I did. I'd heard it all before, and it didn't convince me of anything, except that he wanted to have a lot of sex with me. He told me he hadn't had sex in three months and had dated only two women since his broken engagement two years prior. He was focused on Christianity, but didn't talk about it much, which was good. The last thing I needed was another overzealous religious fanatic.

When I finally get affection and attention, a part of me feels like, *OK, that should hold you for a while. Now you can pay attention to more important things.* It's almost as if it's a food I crave only every couple of months. But a man is not a box of chocolates, and if I treat a man like that, the sex will be no more satisfying than a Godiva dark chocolate truffle. Those are pretty damn good, though. Most men who would go for being a box of chocolates are not looking for love but for a vagina fix. Maybe I wanted marriage, but probably not kids, because they would need constant attention, and I couldn't give that to anyone or anything. But Mike said he wanted kids. "I want you falling in love with me," he breathed, and patted my abdomen. "I want a baby growing in here."

Kids. They would demand the energy I needed for my creative projects. There was also the deep-seated fear of weight gain; I was already too fat. Pregnancy is a drain on the system, not to mention raising a child. The world is overpopulated and polluted, so there is never any logical reason to bring another person into it. I also couldn't see myself as a wife and mother; I was much too much of a free spirit. I would teach, and all of my students would be my children.

So what I was doing with Mike was dangerous. And would it be such a tragedy if I never had an orgasm? How could an orgasm be better than dancing? Looking back, it never has been. Dancing was always better than anything else.

Late one night, after stuffing my anger in the form of muffins because he hadn't called yet, I tormented myself even further. Was he dumping me? *Why* would he go through that entire charade about falling in love, living together, marriage, and babies, only to dump me as soon as I was hooked? What was I? A trout? OK. I got what I wanted: Sex. Attention. But it felt almost as bad as if he had driven up, kidnapped me, raped me, and tossed me in a ditch. Even if he was just in it for sex, why give up the prospect of lots more of it with a woman of my caliber? Unreal. Maybe he did have HIV. My mind conjured up a wide assortment of tools with which to torture itself.

So I decided to pretend nothing ever happened. Mike who? He was just something to tide me over until school started. Obviously, I was just a little spice in his life too, so we were even. I then imagined him driving up and knocking on my window.

He finally called. So I went a little berserk. I just wanted to prepare myself for the worst.

Men have an actual physical need for sex and that disturbs me for some reason. It means I'd better be good at sex if I want a man around, even though all I really want from him is understanding. So I basically have to *use* sex to *get* love, because a man can't seem to love someone with whom he can't have good sex. Yet he can have great sex with someone he doesn't love. I just kept getting more confused on this point. I still am.

He was right about my not being able to let go sexually, which really means emotionally in my book. Enjoying my own pleasure was hard for me. I was trained to be both self-conscious and industrious, so sex is either a performance or it's work. Am I accomplishing anything while having sex? Am I onstage? Unless we're trying to make a baby, it's not exactly constructive. So it's a performance then. OK, and who is my audience exactly? It must be him.

I was inorgasmic because I could not fully trust any man and could never allow myself to need anyone. How could I trust someone with a vastly different set of values and priorities, with a completely different worldview that was usually at odds with my own? There was no way I would ever conform to his way of thinking or even be able to live with it day in and day out for years on end.

Mike had been with twenty or thirty women; he'd had sex only three months ago; he admitted he had hardly ever used a condom; he'd had two broken engagements; and he didn't want me to talk to either of his exes. And I was supposed to be relaxed with this man? I wanted us to travel the road together, but we would have to maintain separate vehicles so I wouldn't feel like I was submerging myself in him. The vulnerability had to be eradicated. Building and maintaining my own identity seemed to mean not only breaking away from my family of origin, but also remaining free from inundation by a man. Even the act of letting him drive felt like I was conceding control to him.

"Wedded bliss" and "true love" are commercially manufactured illusions. Subjecting any man to a life with me would just be cruel and vice versa apparently. If Mike's intentions had not included marriage, I would have been hurt. The fact that they did, scared me. I didn't want the commitment and compromise that marriage would require, but I did want love and monogamy. Only the good stuff, none of the hard stuff, please. Furthermore, why should I take some man's last name? I already had another man's last name, thank you very much. Every last name that exists in the world is some man's name, so the underlying concept of a woman having either her father's or husband's name is still ownership. The children are "stamped" with the "brand" name of the family, as if they are also owned by the man.

Since he was a warmed-over Christian, we eventually started arguing about the Bible stating that the male is to be the controller of the household. This was the ultimate deal breaker. He was judging me according to standards I didn't even acknowledge, let alone adhere to. Drunk Jewish men who have been dead two thousand years telling me how to live my life? I told him we had to be partners in the household—equal in decision-making power. It was around this time that the sex dropped off.

Every time I let my heart go dancing, it came back limping. Maybe I should've just taken the hint again: I wasn't meant to have a relationship with a man. No man could give me what only I could give myself. And let's face it, most men would rather not live in the shadow of a woman who's smarter and more talented than they are, or who is determined to be. So most women have to lower their standards to be with almost any man. The only man I ever met who was sharp did not want marriage, and was then snatched away by a cult. Men who want marriage are usually boring and conventional. The only group they'd join is a bowling league.

17. CONUNDRUM

OK, so just one time, we slipped and skipped the condom. What were the chances? If I got AIDS, it would mean I got it from him and we would spend our last days together. Misery loves company. So does disease. I was trying to be cautious, but obviously not hard enough. I had the pills in my possession, but I was waiting to start them after my period...which never came. As negligent as I was, I could have been much worse. I could have gone on a sex spree, but I didn't, mainly due to the AIDS fear. I didn't even trust condoms. They could break. So we abstained for three weeks straight and still no period.

I dragged myself to Planned Parenthood.

The tests were negative, but no period could mean only one thing. I went to the hospital for a blood test. Mike seemed completely carefree. He wasn't the one who would have to carry a bowling ball in his belly for nine months, undergo public scrutiny, have to quit teaching aerobics, gain weight, have more back problems, deal with parental reaction, lose his freedom, etc. I simply could not accept becoming a slave to my own sexuality by unintentionally becoming eternally attached to another human being. Motherhood was never part of my plans.

Is sex just too animalistic, too much of a distraction? Doesn't it just drain a person's energy for no good reason? Because love is not sex. I'm not sure what it is, but I know what it's not. I don't feel more loved if I have more sex. On the contrary, I usually feel less loved and more used. Sex is a vacuum. Infatuation is blind. But love must have 20/20 vision.

What would happen? I would finish the semester and then stop again? Not go to school during the last trimester and first six months after the birth? A whole year? He thought a woman should stay home and take care of the kids. I wanted to teach, to be out in the world. What about my concert? A pregnant dancer? I couldn't believe that any woman could find complete fulfillment in just being a spouse and parent. What are we—production machinery? What is this species, just a factory for more of the same? Is this Earth even fit for new human beings? We have to look at the big picture, not just our own desires.

I wanted to be loved, not trapped. He seemed to have no empathy for my plight, since he would be getting what he wanted. If I was pregnant, I decided, the relationship would be over.

The lab results came back positive. Next came severe abdominal spasms, shock, and tears. Why? It had all been a hypothetical case until then. There was now the actual knowledge that there was a life growing inside me. I watched the tiny heart beating on the ultrasound monitor, and I started crying again—out of sheer amazement. Suddenly it seemed like the ultimate in creativity.

But Mike quickly went from feeling carefree to feeling trapped. He told me his heart was broken. "This isn't how I wanted it to happen," he stated. There was nothing about my state that made him happy? So where did that leave us? I hated the idea of abortion, but I also hated the idea of being forced into parenthood before I was ready and without a partner who was into it with both feet. I had only a rented room and a bike. There was no health insurance, no place for a baby, no car, and no money. We weren't married, and I wanted to be married first. I wanted it to be special—not rushed. Would he ever get over an abortion? He also hated the concept. Who doesn't? But sometimes it's a wiser choice.

I guess I was already pregnant when I picked up the pills.

The pregnancy made us slow down, of course. If we terminated, the potential human being would not know it. It wasn't conscious; it had only been four weeks; it was barely an embryo. I found myself groping my way through the jungle of controversy surrounding abortion. If carrying it to term was going to hurt the relationship even more than it already had, I didn't want to go through with it. The relationship was just not strong enough to handle a baby. Both would put a strain on us, but an abortion would be less strain than a baby.

What would I have been writing about if I hadn't gotten involved with him? I barely came to terms with one crisis before becoming mired in another. We either had to end a potential life or we had to crush an immature relationship with a child that no one was ready for.

The analysis continued unabated. I told myself *any* life was *not* better than *no* life; *quality* of life was what mattered. Like any self-respecting woman of the nineties, I wanted to be married, happy, and financially secure before I even thought about having a child. He told me he wasn't ready to be a father, which contradicted what he had indicated in bed. He basically turned away from our creation.

Nausea and fatigue followed me around like bowling balls attached to my ankles all day. When I met with the doctor, I prayed he could squeeze it into his schedule that same week. We slated it for the following Monday, October 19th. My birthday.

A bunch of pro-lifers were parading in front of the Boulder Women's Health Center as I drove by on my way to the procedure. I felt like I had to convince everyone that an abortion was the right thing for me to do in my present circumstance.

But this wasn't how I wanted it to be. I had also made the huge mistake of telling my mother, but a young woman cannot go through something like that without sharing it with someone. Of course, she did not keep that information to herself. Let's just say they were "concerned," but they did not disown me at that exact moment. That happened incrementally.

On the morning of October 20th, 1992, I woke up feeling nothing but relief. And it wasn't as bad as all that. For the past week I had felt like I was facing my own crucifixion. I never thought I'd know what that was like. Mike hadn't been there and didn't plan on making an appearance the whole day. A friend from work gave me a ride home. One week I had a family—the next week, nothing.

Men with guns kept chasing me through my dreams. I ran for my life through intricate, unfamiliar properties, kind of like being chased through the recreation building at Michigan again.

Two small

trick or treaters

came to his door tonight.

The little angel

who tried to

pass herself off

as a witch—

poked him

with her green finger.

Seeing him with a child—

now I remember to cry.

I tell him I love him.

He asks, "Are you sure?"

And we both look away

from the empty space.

18. AFTERMATH

He said he felt a "sense of responsibility" toward me as a man who let his lustful urges carry him away and is then consumed with guilt, because he knows he never really loved the woman he said he once did, while in bed with her. He became a zombie. He had offered me everything—love, commitment, marriage, children—and then swiped it all away. I guess he realized he wasn't a fundamentalist Christian after all, and he discovered that I was not as subservient and traditional as he had hoped. I wouldn't ride in the passenger's seat.

What was left to offset the loss? His words? His making dinner for me? He wanted to quit having sex for a while. I couldn't say that I had been 100 percent satisfied with it anyway. Perhaps he had a fear of not being able to satisfy me, and that I would never be satisfied with anything. Early on, he had said he would make that his personal goal. They always say that when I tell them I don't think I've had an orgasm. But he had experienced orgasm and I hadn't. It pissed me off.

How could he love me if he didn't like the workings of my mind? Had my body obscured his view of my soul? Could he separate my personality from my political stance—my liberal inclinations, which he deplored? How can anyone see the mind of a "pretty woman" without getting distracted by the packaging? Why are a woman's looks so ridiculously important? What is the big deal? Am I just an Angry White Pretty Woman struggling to be heard?

In November 1992, Clinton won, and my notebook was almost full. It seemed like the perfect time to make the break with Mike. Until any *man* would be willing to run for *vice* president alongside a female presidential candidate, we still have rampant sexism. Women need to be fully integrated into higher levels of power, not by acting like men but by *not* acting like men. Men already do that just fine. There is never any value in copying something. Yet acting like a *stereotypical* woman is not ideal either. What women know instinctually, men can never learn. The world cannot live on logic alone, but men are certainly not always logical in their decision making, since ego often trumps logic. There is a higher plane of thought and operation that we have not yet approached. And if men are so good at running things... well, need I say more?

The day after the election, he broke it off. He said I suffocated him with all the analysis. "Me thinks thou dost process too much." Perhaps I needed to learn not to pull a relationship up by the roots to see if it's growing. I tried to protect myself by making sure there were no skeletons in the closet, so I spent a lot of time picking bones. On the other hand, it was a good thing I did, else I might have wound up married to a Bible-thumping control freak. We can love each other all we want, but that doesn't mean we can tolerate living together. It's like having the best working parts for a machine, but if they don't fit together, the thing will never operate.

Men are such cowards; they just pretend to be invulnerable. Women have more courage than that. He thought I still wasn't over Steve. Maybe I never would be. Some experiences simply leave a mark on your soul for a lifetime. Now, once again, I had no one distorting my perception of reality, no one to fall back on. Having a man in my life made me lazy. A relationship was a luxury I couldn't afford. After breaking up and crying it out, my vision was clearer. How can anyone be happy if their well-being is in the hands of another? I would never relinquish my progressive attitudes just because they didn't lend themselves to a relationship with a man. What a bitch am I!

As if just because a woman is white and pretty, it is a foregone conclusion that she will not only *want* to set up house with the opposite sex, she is *expected* to do so regardless of how few acceptable partners she finds or how much she begs to differ.

What was I to do but simply forego any type of relationship with a man? What with the AIDS epidemic, one couldn't even safely *kiss* another human being until that person got tested and produced documents with the results and then took a lie detector test to prove he hadn't been with anyone for six months prior to the test. It may or may not be safer to be married, because there is always the issue of trust and fidelity. And divorce is possible at any stage. Absolute monogamy until death is such a rare phenomenon these days that it will be a miracle if society clings to the ideals of marriage very far into the twenty-first century, unless we expand the definition of marriage and family. But I am convinced that men will never care much for monogamy. And I don't think many women care much for it either.

The open-door policy was what I needed all the time. Perhaps I feared commitment, being pigeonholed. What others viewed as stability, I saw as stagnation. Everyone needs to be a hunter sometimes, some of us more than others. There had to be obstacles to overcome, no clear path, a sense of possibility—or even better, impossibility. Seemingly impossible goals were particularly appealing to me. And why make promises you are not sure you can keep?

Again, it went back to me feeling like an alien in American culture. After a period of trying to fit in somehow, knowing all the while that I was not being true to myself, I always seemed to wind up back outside the constructs of society, like a solitary tree amid a row of houses or a wolf among refrigerators. Perhaps it was due to growing up in the middle of nowhere or not having any sisters to teach me how to be a girl, but the traditional female role was just not working out for me. And perhaps it was all for the best. Deep down, I knew I did not want that role. I wanted to write my own script.

19. STANDARDS

There was one more bad man experience in store for me in Boulder. This one (we'll call him Rob), at thirty-seven, drove a Jeep (not a Cherokee) all year long, meaning the legs would freeze while riding in the thing in winter. As an upstart documentary filmmaker, he was schmoozing for money at every turn. Having lived in Aspen for a time, he knew some Richie Riches and was mounting a fundraising campaign for transforming an old dairy into a center for the arts, which I found attractive. He wore his Frenchie hat backward to cover his balding head and had pudgy Filipino cheeks that gave him that cool, artsy chipmunk look.

Initially, he appeared simply superior to me. He was "ahead" of me because he was running his own business in the field he wanted to be in. Even though I was much younger than all the men in my life (all baby boomers), I always felt I was competing with them. The power struggle began after "Hi, nice to meet you." Or even before that, in who spoke first.

So he reinforced my inferiority complex through constant evaluation. He hurled verbal knives at me when supposedly drunk. Sometimes I would repeat to him some of the things he said, and he would be dumbfounded. "I said that?" he would ask in disbelief, and then he would laugh.

Reminded me of someone. Was I really reenacting my relationship with my father in all my relationships? I listed what I disliked about this specimen and what I disliked about my father, and the lists were indeed the same. My father's approval was always conditional. His support carried a price tag. I was left with the burden of proof—to *prove* to him that what I was doing was valid, significant, and a potentially commercial endeavor. And that's what I had to do with Rob.

Rob's moods varied wildly from day to day. It was back to walking around on eggshells. He had so many rules regarding his dwelling place, even though it was just someone's basement, and I was *always* at *his* place. He lived on the north side of town and I was on the south side when we met, so I moved into a room with some Buddhists on a quiet street close to Rob's. But he wouldn't give me a key to his place because that "implied too much commitment."

He said there was so much he wanted to tell me but felt he couldn't. That was like telling me there were so many treasures behind a certain door, but he wouldn't open it for me. I was supposed to find the key in a haystack.

He was doing his thing and I wasn't. Frustration defined my life, and he put me down for feeling frustrated. If he couldn't even accept my feelings as valid, what was he? When things went well for him, I felt worse about myself.

I had lost my center, and it seemed the only way I could get back to it was by isolating myself from those who would judge me—which was everybody.

I hated the political who-knows-whom crap that defined the schmoozing snooty Boulder arts community. I wanted to accomplish my goals *alone* or not at all. Being around people made me tense; I couldn't be myself. Everyone else had more money than I did, and I didn't want to be influenced by anyone, let alone feel like I had to kiss ass. Everyone Rob knew was rich or influential or knew someone who was. It was all ego-play, like some mini-Hollywood in the mountains. I just wanted to lock myself up and write, like Emily Dickinson. So what if no one read a word I wrote until after my demise? At least I would be spared the torture of this twisted comparison-fest.

Rob didn't even sit next to me when he was showcasing his video at some guy's house, probably because he didn't see me as good for his "star" image. He complained that I didn't want to "take advantage" of his connections. When I said I felt like I was trying to catch up with him, he sneered and said, "You haven't even caught up with what I did when I was twenty-five." While feeling like an outsider as he was mingling, I justified it with, "Well, you've been in Boulder three times as long as I have, so of course you know more people than I do." He countered with, "I knew more people here after one year than you do now."

Instead of saying I had good ideas, he told me that I had too many ideas and that we needed people to implement ideas, not generate more. When I took steps toward implementation, he criticized my tactics. We both had oversized egos. He told me I gave him "too much power" by telling him I loved him. So the power corrupted him. As if love is a matter of power, not of the heart.

I couldn't tell whether I was flying forward or falling backward as I became more enmeshed in Boulder. I discovered, however, that I didn't care about joining any crowd, not even the so-called artistic highbrow club. My background was entirely notwithstanding. What I'd gained since leaving my home state were tools for survival as an artist, the primary tool being a thicker skin.

Did I truly love the man, or did I just love what he was "about"? He said I needed more self-confidence, but he never built me up, and whenever I built myself up, he told me I was being self-centered. He didn't want me to give him the power, but he took it anyway. It appeared that it was high time for a little undercover work again.

After seeking out and meeting a recent ex-girlfriend of his, I found out he had lied about how much time had elapsed between her and me. He downplayed everything that happened between them, because she had actually made him face up to his character flaws. It turned out that he was looking for a mother who never criticized him and was stronger than him, both emotionally and financially. So I had confirmation of my preliminary analysis.

Any woman who was going to be with him had to:

- be independently wealthy (since he wasn't)
- do something socially responsible (looks good in Boulder)
- be beautiful (since he was ugly)
- be a great socialite (but not overshadow him)
- not change her mind too much (but think his way)
- be into the arts (but not more than him)
- have a scientific mind (but not be smarter than him)
- be very orderly (but not anal)
- not talk about herself too much (it would take the focus off him)
- dress in a way that pleases him (not herself) and
- be totally supportive of *him* (and need no support herself).

The fog was clearing; I was finally starting to see the truth about him—and my father. My father was angry about everything, but mostly about his mom, his sister, and his wife, because they didn't let him have his way 100 percent of the time. I was angry about how his anger poisoned the family. There had been nothing but arguments ever since I could remember. So I learned early on that this is how a man and a woman interact: they constantly argue and never resolve anything. My father accepted *no* responsibility for anything; he just assigned blame elsewhere. Just like Rob.

Rob would say, "I don't care if you're living in the gutter, as long as you're doing what you want." Then he would proceed to complain about my lack of money. It boiled down to the fact that I didn't have the kind of income he wanted his girlfriend to have—so he could sponge off her. He was obviously insecure about his place—a basement. Part of him felt inadequate due to *his* lack of substantial income, but his alter ego would yodel about being a "socialist" and having to "walk his talk."

Perhaps it was when he saw me blowing bubbles at my brother's wedding that he finally decided to let me go. Blowing bubbles at a wedding? Why not? I was getting reacquainted with my ten-year-old self. I liked myself better at that age.

He was a nice guy? He didn't mean to use women? He was unaware of what he was doing? I wasn't so sure. Everyone I spoke to, including Rob himself, told me he was bad news when it came to relationships. He was always keeping score. And I had to match the coordinates of his ideal woman. But only the ideal matches the ideal, not the human. He broke it off by saying, "I don't want to be mean to you anymore."

Does the fear of loneliness equal the desire to be with someone? People do get married for security—just to know that someone is there, as a kind of safety net of sorts. Did I simply fear being without him? Was I weak because I needed reinforcement? He never answered that question. It seemed that he was weak, since his ego always needed a boost, always needed a cheerleader.

It seems the only way men boost the ego of women is by telling them they're beautiful. Does a man often have a crush on a woman because he loves how smart, talented, and ethical she is? Does a man gush "You are *so* smart" on a first date? Does he comment on her impressive educational background? Why do women love to hear a man tell them they're beautiful? Is beauty the full measure of a woman's power?

Someone came back from Tibet, and I had to leave the lovely Buddhist enclave behind. I then found a place with another single mom in Lafayette, one of the nearby outlying towns. I was grateful it was closer to I-25, since I was commuting to school in Greeley, Colorado. After getting to know my new roommate and finding out how difficult her life was, I imagined how much more treacherous my life and the life of my child would have been if I had become a single mom. This made me consider getting my tubes tied. That might have mitigated some of my fears at that point. But I ran the idea past my mother, of course, and she started crying. So I put the idea to rest for the time being.

Yes, I was still driving the nerve-racking Nova and going to school throughout both the Mike and the Rob quagmires. I was getting ready for student teaching and preparing my second theatrical production in Boulder. But half of me felt like I was just shuffling around, putting off the one big risk that terrified me: Going to Hollywood. Either you Get a Job, Get Married, and Have Kids, or you Go to Hollywood. Or you join a cult. It appears there really aren't that many options in life after all.

20. A KICK IN THE HEAD

After having undergone all my teacher training at very white colleges in Colorado, yet having gone to high school in that integrated small town, I felt I was ready for the challenge of student teaching in colorful inner-city Denver. Only it wasn't so colorful. It was just one color. My professors tried to dissuade me from such an undertaking, but I was adamant. Besides, the school housed not only the junior high but also a magnet school of the arts, so I thought it would be like *Fame*. Perhaps they would let me teach a few dance classes and even choreograph some routines.

So I was placed with a black woman who had been teaching seventh grade for over twenty years. She dressed impeccably in business attire, wore dentures, and had hair that was tidy and always conservatively coiffured. The first question she asked me was, "Have you had any experience working with African American students?" When I told her that I had attended high school with them, she wasn't impressed, and she launched into a lecture explaining how black students were "different" than white students, how it was tougher to teach in the inner city than anywhere else, how I had to be on my guard and could never relax, because I was in the "hood" now. She wanted to make me sweat. And sweat I did.

This woman was all about regimens, rows of seats, routines, and dittos. There was no discussion of Maya Angelou's poetry, no debate on the socioeconomic status of African Americans, no essays on *To Kill a Mockingbird*. But I bravely put together a lesson plan using one of Angelou's poems, rearranged the seats in a circle for discussion—and those kids made an immediate connection with the drug trade. It was the poem entitled *Alone*. They wondered aloud about whether they could sell drugs on their own and get away with it or if they needed help or if they could make it some other way on their own, without the gangs. This was their world. These were their choices. But this was deemed "inappropriate subject matter" and was not at all condoned by their teacher. The open-ended discussion that floored me was cut short, and it was back to rows, routines, and dittos.

She later told me that leaving things too open-ended invited chaos in the classroom and that the kids needed constant structure. I had to believe what she was telling me, yet I felt uncomfortable with her demeanor. She was telling me what my attitude had to be if I was going to survive this ultimate test, and one thing I cannot tolerate is someone telling me what my attitude should be.

I was anxious to get to know the students, to try innovative teaching methods, and to motivate them to express themselves through the English language. But with her, it was the classroom management drumbeat ad nauseam. I didn't realize that my primary task during this final phase of preparing to help steer the next generation toward developing their full potential was to act as this woman's shadow for ten weeks. Me? Someone else's shadow?

Being distraught over what was transpiring on the academic side of the building, my attempts at choreography on the artistic side were rather scattered, but I did notice that the arts students were more focused and intense in their work. Another glaring difference was that all of them were white. It was literally night and day when crossing over from one side of the facility to the other. And no one seemed too concerned about classroom management on the artistic side. The kids had talent. Years later that school moved on to its own location and has since become quite successful.

But my "experience" at the school only lasted four weeks, before she just wanted me out of her classroom. The two of us were completely different in our approaches and had wildly divergent views on fundamental issues in education. I was told I was "still a student" on the one hand, but on the other I was supposed to demonstrate authority. I was told I could not get to know the students because that would "undermine my authority." I was told that routine and structure were the only ways to maintain order in the classroom. All of this flew in the face of everything I believed and had been taught about teaching—about education. Little did I know, I had been taught methods that are used primarily in white suburban schools. Apparently, there is a yawning chasm between the two. And the whole time, I had to wonder how it would have turned out if I had been a male in the same situation. Or black.

So there I was—student loans mounting, the past three years spent in pursuit of a teaching certificate, not to mention three traumatic dead-end relationships, and I was cut short of getting the credential I needed because I had gone for a challenge.

The college told me it was too late in the semester for them to find me another situation, and "by the way, it looks like you're missing a few classes here." They blamed me for the failure, and I was livid. The system had failed me. I decided that public school teaching was not for me, at least not at the time.

I didn't just want to teach, I wanted to work for reform. I knew that even though the bureaucracy and the parents may not want people like me, the kids did. I decided that someday I would start an alternative school and show them how it should be done. But at that time, I was just glad I had the chance to throw all my energy into my theater production that was going up in four weeks. There were even two ten-year-old girls in the show, and they were the best performers I ever could have hoped for. So perhaps the production itself served as an alternative school.

21. BEAUTY IS A LIQUID ASSET

My parents came to the show and were supportive, and after the show was over, my dad bought me a 1979 Toyota Corolla for a couple thousand bucks. Still no AC, but a decided improvement. They tried to talk me into coming home, but I would have none of it.

"But what are you going to do now?"

I told them I had started working with a modeling agency in Denver, just print and commercial stuff—no fashion, since I was not built like a reed. Hollywood would be next summer, definitely, but I did not tell them about that plan. If I stayed grounded, I figured that would keep me from thinking that the entertainment industry was more important than education or the farm. But I quickly became desperate for another way to make some fast cash, so I scanned the classified ads, and one of them caught my eye:

Uninhibited women and couples
wanted for video project
Make $$$ an hour
Call Danny at XXX-XXXX

The word *uninhibited* with dollar signs close by attracted my attention. Of course I knew it could be a scam—possibly even a dangerous ad to mess with. The guy could be a rapist or something. But I answered the ad, just to prove to myself that I had the guts to do it. I also moved in with my ex-boyfriend, Jake, to save rent money. This went against my better judgment, but a girl has to get by. A step backward, but only so I could leap forward in due time.

As it turned out, not only did I have the nerve to disrobe for a camera, I had quite the flair for exhibitionism. The "filmmaker's" name was Danny and he was a nice guy as far as I could tell, polite and professional. I felt perfectly comfortable in my body and in front of this stranger. He simply had me lie nude on blankets and pillows, then turned on some music, and asked me to move provocatively, so my dance background actually came in handy—kind of a transfer of skills. It made sense to me to move in an animalistic way; my wild side again had an outlet. Here was a situation where that side of me was actually desired.

He paid me well for the shoot and did not expect anything else.

After the project, he encouraged me to audition at some of the topless clubs in Denver. What did I have to lose? Except my clothes. I was tired of them anyway. Even though Jake had teased me about how I could make some money off my lovely "rack," he was none too thrilled about my calling his bluff.

"I don't want other men looking at you like that," he stated.

"Like what?" I asked.

I was determined to do whatever it took, short of anything illegal, to survive on my own. I could not go back to my parents' farm and their claustrophobic, rigid attitudes. I had come too far to turn back. It was kind of my *Thelma and Louise* moment.

The world beyond their plot of land went way beyond their dim memory of bygone days. Their knowledge had become mostly an ingrained belief system. But they had taught me to be a nonconformist and that meant not conforming to them either. So their approach sort of backfired. Up until then, I had always told them the hard truth about everything, but after I switched career tracks, that had to stop. It was the end of an era, the end of my childhood at twenty-eight.

I went at my own pace through life.

I slinked into an upscale club in Denver with the determination to throw caution to the wind. Armed with a red cape, glued-on nails, two-inch black pumps, and lingerie from Victoria's Secret, I teetered up onto the platform with about five men around it and danced franticly to music that was way too fast. As I ripped off my bra, I had the fleeting feeling that Mom would actually be proud of my liberation. And history was made for me. The club manager, however, could see that I was a bit too green for that establishment. So I traipsed over to a more middle-class joint. They took me in.

Getting a major injection of attention every day was a boon to my self-image. Any place that included a stage and music was perfect for me. The manager explained how table dances were done, on a pedestal at least six feet from the customer, upstairs away from the main floor. As I went along, I became more adventurous and more comfortable with expressing my sexuality. It even made sex more exciting, so Jake and I enjoyed each other even more. I made more money in one night than I did in a week working at the preschool or the deli. It seemed to be a great way to take care of myself instead of spending all my energy trying to solve America's social problems. On the other hand, it bothered me that the job was devoid of social benefit and would certainly not look good on a resume. So I told myself it was only a financial stepping stone to the artistic career that I had been aiming for, like it is for every young female artist in similar circumstances.

But then my anxiety complex stepped in and asked what would happen if I was still dancing at thirty-five or forty. Would I be able to compete with the younger girls? What kind of background is exotic dancing? Isn't it just the first rung on the descending career ladder into the sex industry (the last rung being "professional")? If I couldn't tell my mother about it, maybe it wasn't such a good idea. But my mom was an old prude, I argued with myself, not open-minded about anything sexual. Then there was my body image complex caused by years of going to dance classes with prepubescent ballet babies.

I was more like a brunette Marilyn Monroe, not the ideal by today's standards and basically fat in the world of professional dance. But erotic dance was far removed from modern dance. Wonder of wonders, men actually liked to see some evidence of femaleness. The fashion industry had invented the "bones as clothes rack" concept. Designers want people to notice their work, not the female flesh underneath it.

The fact is, we are more like animals than we like to acknowledge, perhaps because animals don't build big houses or drive cars like we do. Mainstream America still does not think it's socially acceptable for a woman to have a multitude of sex partners, yet many men feel marriage is a trap. What's a woman to do with her healthy sex drive? And a woman with little money who marries a man with big money is also looked down upon. She's just a gold digger. What exactly should she be digging for—rusty nails? Men have always dug for gold, and would never waste time and energy digging for anything that was not a highly sought after commodity.

So a beautiful woman with a high degree of sensuality and a bit of exhibitionism who needs to make money quickly, needs to avoid debt, and hasn't found an acceptable mate (or "sugar daddy")—what should she do? Most men, if they were in that situation as a beautiful woman, would not hesitate one second to enter into adult entertainment or even prostitution. Men are still freer to follow their instincts without being stigmatized or held to ridiculous standards that make no sense. As a matter of fact, they can actually gain notoriety for being known womanizers. Only in places like Vegas, Paris, Hollywood, and New York City is it sort of acceptable for women to assert their full sexual power and freedom, but even then they are still seen as loose city women to conservatives and the folks back home on Main Street who would categorize *Sex and the City* as smut. Too bad for them.

I was earning a living in a very distinctive way, but no one is the equivalent of what they do to pay the bills. So much of the socioeconomic categorizing that goes on in America is entirely nonproductive and dehumanizing. Furthermore, there are major job skills involved in topless dancing: interpersonal skills, physical stamina, withstanding a crummy work environment, managing a variable income, tolerating bitchy dancers and asshole managers, and the ability to smile through it all. A stint in the skin trade, I figured, would leave me well prepared for anything, just so long as it did not devolve into something more illicit or outright illegal. I had my reputation to consider.

During the novice day shift at the middle-class club, I had been doing my job as I understood it. Every man who walked into the place I considered fair game. After all, I had to make money; otherwise there was no reason to waste my time and my lungs just being there.

One day I was entertaining three older men at their table with my sterling personality, feeling sparkly, high on my newfound ability to make cash just by being sexy. Soon I suggested a table dance and managed to get two dances out of one guy. After we returned to their table downstairs, "Zha Zha" came skipping over and asked the same guy if he was ready for a dance, as if they were well acquainted.

"Oh, I'm sorry, I already had a dance—with River here."

Her face fell. She plunked down across from me and glared.

"How much do you work out?" she asked me.

"Almost every day."

"You don't look like it. Look at my bicep." She flexed her arm and the men acted impressed. Clearly, I needed to do more upper body work, but I just smiled and continued on in my merry way, ignoring her.

One of the men asked me, trying to break the tension, "So what did you do before you started dancing?"

"I taught preschool. Before that I was in school—majored in dance and studied English in grad school. Someday you'll all be in my bestseller."

"So you're a writer?"

"That's what I like to think, but I'm still concentrating on dance, as you can see. Only now I'm actually making money doing it."

A few moments later I discovered that one of the men was an accountant. I had my paycheck in my purse, and I had a question about some of the taxes withheld, so I pulled it out to ask him about it as Zha Zha looked on.

Back in the dressing room with all the dancers, she glowered at me from the far end of the row of mirrors—the side reserved for dancers with seniority—and announced, "You know, River, you really don't look like you belong here. Why don't you just go work at Whiskies or something?"

Again, I held my peace and ignored her.

Before my shift the next day, I was called into the manager's office, accused of soliciting, and given the boot. Did Zha Zha have anything to do with that?

22. STEPPING OFF

The working class club was located along an industrial stretch, a bit further west and actually closer to Boulder. Opening the door, I ducked into the dark cave. Standing under a low ceiling while my eyes adjusted to the near blackness, I instinctively began nose-breathing, taking in only small sniffs of what oxygen there was. The smell was a mix of cheap toilet cleaner, beer, and cigarette smoke. The music hit my head like a sledgehammer. To my right was the bar, to my left was the DJ booth, and there was one large stage and three smaller ones, all at eye level with the customer. So this was the place she told me to work, as an insult. But it was adapt or die at that point. There wasn't much choice.

Even in that dive, I still made money—not as much as before, but still way better than preschool pay. Every dollar was a vote for me in my political arena: my stage. It was just a "stage" club and no table dances at all, but being eye level with the customers helped to generate more lucrative "sets". There is so much power in female energy, in eroticism itself, and nothing is more persuasive than a beautiful, sensual woman. It's the best of everything embodied.

I had been making my way around the bar, spouting intellectual and political diatribes just to get reactions. One man turned his head to smile at me, someone I thought I had seen once before. He held out a twenty-dollar bill like a carrot, and I took the bait, silly rabbit that I was.

"Now, why is a beautiful, intelligent woman like you not married?"

I smiled sheepishly at this typical question, but this time it wasn't so typical, given the way this man smiled at me and his mellow tone of voice.

"Well, maybe I really don't want to be married. I've passed on two chances already. And besides, I'm pretty much impossible."

"Impossible? You couldn't be as impossible as my ex-wife. I'm telling you, I will never marry again. I couldn't take another chance on this happening again." He proceeded to relay his story, being completely open with me, telling me about her affair, how he found out about it, how they agreed to enter into counseling for the sake of the kids. And how she served him with papers on his 44th birthday.

A nasty custody battle ensued, and he took off and stayed in a hotel for two weeks.

After he had unloaded all of this, he thanked me for listening, gave me his card, and left the premises. He had been polite and warm, different from the typical customer.

I liked him. Yes, I was still living with Jake and felt guilty about being attracted to this man, but Jake and I had not been very intimate as of late, due to our wildly divergent work schedules. Three days later, I tried calling. When his five-year-old daughter answered, I felt as if I'd just bumped into an occupied bathroom stall. She inadvertently hung up on me.

I was crest-fallen.

Four days later, I had just finished on stage four, and he was there. I sidled up to the stool next to him while he was talking to a waitress. Under the table, his hand found mine and squeezed it tenderly, and then he pressed a twenty into my sweaty palm. I returned the grasp automatically. There was an undertow at work, and I was being pulled into it. But the problem was where we had met. How could I be sure that he wasn't just trying to fulfill his stripper fantasy? But all those months of working as a dancer in that barren desert suddenly seemed like the price I paid for finally meeting this man. He had emerged like a mirage. After apologizing for his daughter, we chatted for a bit, and then he asked me out.

He made me feel—again—how much I wanted and needed something my life just didn't seem to leave room for. There was the constant searing pain of needing to merge completely with him, alongside the deep knowledge that it wasn't possible.

Most dancers are biding their time, waiting to marry their worthless boyfriends. Then there are those who think they are lesbians or may actually be lesbians. They hate men, usually because a man abused them or abandoned them at a critical moment. And, of course, there are the princesses who are waiting for their knight in shining armor to come galloping into the club to sweep them off their six-inch heels. I did not really know which subset I fit into. Apparently none of the above.

Before I realized how hard it was to keep up the act, I used to think that being an "entertainer" was like mooching off society, using your looks to get what you want out of poor, unsuspecting men. Yeah, right, the poor guys. Many great men have met their downfall through the femme fatale. Well, more power to us, as long as we ultimately use our power for some social good, because clearly the money being tossed around a strip club is not going to any good use. It needs to be properly re-purposed.

But there is the endless keeping up of appearances, facades, and attitudes, day after day, week after week, month after month—and how did any girl make it through a whole year without having a nervous breakdown? Well, drugs, that's how. But I never went there, choosing instead to do yoga and take a road trip every once in a while.

Men are unable to keep their hands out of the proverbial cookie jar of beautiful women. So we have an entire industry built on the cookie jar concept—trying to tempt men to reach into the cookie jar, which is constantly being replenished with new generations of women. Manipulation of men has risen to an art form. Over time, I refined this highly specialized skill by getting in closer touch with my basic instincts and by scrutinizing men in their natural habitat. Many of them are simply there to get some cheap psychotherapy "under the table," so to speak. They can talk to us about things that "real men" never mention out in the jungle of the business world or to their wives.

I arrived first and waited for him in the lobby. He saw me as soon as he entered. He smiled sweetly, genuinely, and escorted me to the bar and bought me a glass of wine. He immediately started talking about his boys and how they were glad he was getting out, but also how they were slightly worried about him.

After we were seated, he went to call them just to make sure everything was all right. Watching him talk to them on the phone warmed my core. Here was a man who was primarily concerned about his children. As he transmuted into the kind of father figure I had always imagined, he was elevated to a level above angels. The meal tasted heavenly while in the company of such divinity.

"I want you to know that I'm not after sex. This is the first time I've gotten out since the divorce. I just had this feeling about you. You're obviously educated and working a job that's way below your intellectual skills. But you're also absolutely gorgeous, and you know it."

"Well, if I'm so smart, why am I in debt?"

"We're all in debt. But dancing the way you do, you won't be for long. You must do pretty well for yourself."

"It's OK." I shoveled a bite of Buddha's delight into my mouth. It was the first real meal I'd had in weeks. He watched me silently for a moment.

"Have you ever been made love to—properly?"

I blushed. I chewed. I took a drink. "I um—don't believe I've ever had an orgasm, so I guess the answer is no. But that's probably because I just don't know my body well enough to be able to teach anybody what to do." I laughed nervously.

"If you want to teach me, I'd be a willing student."

I looked at him askance. "I thought you weren't after sex."

"I'm not. I was just offering." He grinned.

"Well, like I said, I don't know how to teach anyone.

I don't exactly know what's going on down there."

He laughed. "I just can't believe you don't have a man in your life."

"Well, I am living with an ex-boyfriend—temporarily. I'm just trying to save enough money to get to California."

"Really? I drive to LA every week."

I put down my fork and sipped my wine, peering at him over the rim.

"Would you like to come along with me sometime?"

After driving separately to the movie theater, we found nothing playing that appealed to us. We went to a small bar inside the mall. He told me he had been a regular at the club for six years. I wondered if his wife ever knew. He talked about his wife's affair and his kids. I listened patiently as if we were still at the club and he was getting his free counseling.

We left the theater and walked in silence to the parking lot, both of us afraid to make eye contact at that point. I even began to doubt his attraction to me. After we got to my car, I couldn't take it anymore, so I initiated a hug. He hugged me back, and that was it. He smiled at me and turned to go. I watched him walk away. I got into my car. And the world dropped out from under me.

About halfway back to Boulder, tears welled up. I realized how lonely I was. Jake and I were not building a future together; he was just a pit stop on the way to California, and I was just his roommate with benefits. This new man was...

I stopped at an overlook and gazed out at the lights below. He was the right man at the wrong time. Perhaps there never would be a right time. Or a right man. Or I would never be the right woman. In my life of self-imposed exile and far-flung adventures, a stable relationship seemed outside my realm. But no one had ever been so kind to me. He had asked me questions that I hadn't even gotten around to asking myself. I still believed in love, and I wanted to love, but I couldn't figure out how to love without getting broken.

I missed him the very next day, so I called him and then wound up driving to his place in Longmont, which took over an hour. We watched a movie and what happened afterward I can't recall, but I do recall waking up in his bed.

Jake started getting weird after I told him I had met someone else. Can't imagine why. As my departure for California drew near, he fell more in love with me each day and tried to act like he thought someone in love would act.

I tried to be as kind as possible to him, but I sensed this was all an act on his part. We had ceased intimacy well before I met the truck driver.

23. WASTELAND

Talk about fearless. I took him up on his offer of a ride to LA. There I was, a small-town girl from Michigan taking off in a big rig with a man she met at a Denver strip club only two weeks prior. I just had a bit of the gypsy in my blood. Drifter. Vagabond. Rambler. Yep, that's me. Fearless. No question.

We had a hard time getting over Wolf Creek Pass. It was November, and ice had formed at that altitude, but he was determined to take that route. We stopped to put on chains and have sex before we powered up the incline. After many miles of nothingness, we arrived in Diamond Bar, California, and stopped for a bite and a shower. We arrived at the loading dock in downtown Los Angeles in the wee hours of the morning and had sex before he took a snooze. Sitting in the passenger's seat of his Kenworth with him asleep in the cab, I scrawled about my experience in my notebook. He wasn't the most well-endowed of men, but he made up for it in other ways.

I decided it was time for me to test the sands as a dancer in the desert mirage I'd heard so much about. So on the return trip to Colorado, we enjoyed our last supper together at Denny's next to the Motel 6 in Vegas. After he departed for his big rig, I settled into my quaint hotel room and again entertained grandiose thoughts and danced naked in front of the mirror like the queen of everything.

Las Vegas—represented by stadiums of hungry, hollow, bottomless slots and enough secondhand smoke to choke a hippo. Even the mechanics of a slot machine are a metaphor for a spiritual drainage ditch. The next day, after touring all the topless clubs in the city on foot and ending up diminished and insecure, I felt an overwhelming need to get away from the city. I consulted a map, took a bus, and hiked to the edge of the lights.

I scrambled up the red rocks and came to a plateau, where scruffy weeds, bent by the relentless canyon winds, poked out from between the rocks. After staking out a vantage point, I looked out at the miles and miles of lights proclaiming the downfall of humanity. These were the lights that beckon those who have no alternatives left, those who have sold out, and are now convinced that life and death are encompassed in the roll of the dice, in the pull of a handle, in the stripping down to the bones. The American Wasteland. A Sahara of the Soul.

And what can I say about those dear people who hand out those lovely brochures that promote the buffet of services available in Las Vegas? There's such a wide array from which to choose, how could anyone ever decide? The purveyors of such uplifting entertainment merely stand and hold out their wares to everyone who passes by, women and children included. They are mute: eyes blank, lips sewn shut.

They need some sort of script:

> "Hi! Welcome to Las Vegas!
You look like you need a lovely
female to accompany you on your
wild escapade. I mean, not that your
adorable wife, er—mother—
whatever, here wouldn't go along for
the ride, but I'm sure you could
find some way to ditch her for a while,
so you can go out and have some *real*
fun. I mean, let's be honest—
you came to Vegas for
the sex and the money—
the two go hand in hand here.
So step right up
and grab a piece of the action."

They'd go for that, wouldn't they?

My trucker came back a week later. He just listened as I relayed my lackluster experience of the place, while he was probably thinking that I would lose interest in him too within a few months. He tried to keep me hanging on by feeding me flattery, raving about my body parts and physical aptitudes.

But after not seeing him for a week, I told him I missed him, and he said, "To be honest, Mandy, I haven't even had time to miss you." At that instant, his voice quit sounding like music.

I knew I'd lost my perspective and had to regain the high ground once again. Out of sight, out of mind. Yet when I did think of him, it took my breath away.

Living with a man without paying rent was something I had, as a rule, avoided. But I had made an exception to that rule for almost seven months by that point. I could see that I did enrich and enliven Jake's life, and not just in bed. I had underestimated the value a woman can have in a man's life. I just wanted to avoid having my own self-worth determined by how valuable I was to a man, especially if the value was based primarily on my sexuality. Perhaps I was too sensitive on that issue—or not sensitive enough.

Hadn't I survived on my own long enough to prove whatever I thought I had to prove? Wasn't this a fool's errand? Nothing would ever convince my father of anything. Did I really want to live alone forever? I needed solitude to write, but I also needed balance, someone to be with at the end of the day, some feeling of actually belonging somewhere, sometimes, but I hated admitting that I needed anything or anyone. Attempting to fulfill certain needs seemed futile.

So what else could I do but simply ignore and bury any so-called needs? My own complexity got in the way, and besides, who wants to admit vulnerability? I'd always thought that most men wanted to be with a strong woman anyway—but not too strong. Not stronger than him. But I wanted to be stronger. The only way to be permanently stronger than *him* was not to be with him at all.

24. HOLLYWOOD RUNAWAY

One night I came back to the house around the usual time—midnight. I let myself in, collapsed on the sofa, and began my nightly ritual of dumping out and counting my cash on the coffee table. Jake came down the stairs and coldly revealed that he had a friend spending the night with him upstairs, but he claimed there was "nothing sexual going on." He grabbed a beer from the fridge and went back upstairs. I sat and stared out the window, then went out on the deck and listened to the wind blow through the canyon.

I knew he did it to spite me, because of my escapades, and that was the only way he knew how to express his feelings about the situation. We were absolutely done.

I slept on the couch.

The next morning he told me they would probably have sex if she came up again. At that moment, I felt homeless. I had gotten so used to the warm feeling I had when I came home and knew he was there and I was safe and away from everything. Now there was nowhere to run, nowhere to hide, and I was kicking myself for not having had my own place by then.

I didn't have enough money to go anywhere for three more weeks. I guess I deserved it, because I had started to take the whole situation for granted—him and his place. I'd obviously overstayed my welcome. He even mumbled something about having some sort of right to have sex with me since he let me stay with him. What did that make me?

Not many Middle American parents have ever favored the idea of their only daughter running off to Hollywood. Even after I told myself that Hollywood is only a state of mind built on a sandy fault line, I had to go. I had to become another California runaway, to be part of the hype that makes everyone think that all the Somebodys of the World are out there, and the rest of us are just schmucks—so far from the cutting edge of anything that we are rendered completely inconsequential. It's all a matter of perspective.

On December 6th, 1994, with some twenties under the front seat and about a thousand crumpled dollar bills stuffed in a shoe box in the back seat, I pulled out of Jake's driveway as the first snow swirled about me. I wound my way down the mountain for what I believed was the last time. Where would I go when I stopped being a captive of my past?

I drove south on I-25, basked in the sun across the southwest on I-40, and landed at my cousin's house in San Diego. She was protective of me and let me rest there for a few days. She did not tell her Navy husband about my chosen occupation. Not exactly "connecting" with the conservative clubs of San Diego, which required pantyhose, I quickly worked my way north and found a little club in Norwalk, an industrial stretch east of LA. They took me in.

The club was tame, working-class, fairly safe, and the managers were actually friendly. Two of them were older women who had been managing the place for years. There was one stage with two levels. A dancer could only take off her top on the higher stage that was six feet from the customers. Apparently, there was a six foot rule in many topless clubs at the time, I guess because they figured no guy could reach that far. Instead of table dances, there were chair dances at eye level and up close, but no contact was allowed and tops stayed on.

Sitting at the bar, I was petrified before my first round onstage, and then I spent the first week hiding in the dingy dressing room. I seriously considered driving back home to Michigan, thinking maybe I really had wandered too far from home this time. But then I loosened up and met a dancer named Darcy who wore a bell around her neck and a garter around her somewhat chunky thigh. She took an interest in me when I started asking around about an apartment within driving distance, as I was still driving from a place my cousin had found for me in Oceanside. It just so happened that Darcy had an arrangement for me in a house in Arcadia.

She took me under her wing and showed me the ropes. Before long, I was vamping it up like nobody's business. Merging with the scene, I had a fine time of it, pulling down twice the money I had made back in Colorado. The girls back there were wrong; they'd told me if I didn't like Vegas, I would hate California, but I had no problem with the place.

The house in Arcadia was somewhat hidden from the street with overgrown trees and vegetation, and there were beloved pets in the back room who had endowed the place with fleas. It was owned by an astounding sixty-plus-year-old woman who worked as an extra in Hollywood and had affairs with camera grips. She was somewhat behind on the mortgage payments, so my money came in handy.

Darcy turned out to be a bona fide lesbian who had spent ten years in "the business," including dancing in Vegas. She was instrumental in helping me adapt to Hollywood. We would plunk down in front of *The Tonight Show* after work, and she would unfold another tale of her exploits in Vegas or a harrowing experience with her stepfather or her lackluster agent.

Within two months, I met Gary at the club. He was from San Diego and had that hot frat boy look, even though he was thirty-seven and recently divorced. He said I had "good energy and good proportions" and asked me to lunch at a nearby café, and I accepted, with a few reservations. But I got over them.

When we sat down to lunch, I felt like we were squaring off; the battle lines were being drawn on the table. I wanted to see if I could match wits with him, but my attraction to him was a huge distraction. My temperature skyrocketed just from hearing his voice, even though he was one of those guys who called *everyone* by a pet name. It was "buddy" if referring to a guy; "sweetie," "baby," or "hon" if a woman. Mike did that: "OK, babe." Drove me nuts.

My goal was to keep my sanity, to remain objective and aloof. Most men could not possibly see me as marriage material, so I had to get used to noncommittal men coming on strong and then losing interest soon after the kill or the rejection. I told him that I was not a pushover, that I refused to drown in a river of smooth lines, and that I didn't care for casual sex. I had better things to do than waste time and energy on some idiot male looking for an easy lay. A lot of good that did. He invited me to come see his beach house in La Jolla, and of course I went for it.

A cigarette between his fingers and the image would have been complete. He was posing outside the coffee shop in La Jolla as the living image of the cool Californian. He did not alter his pose even microscopically as I approached him, giving away not one ounce of power. He kept his sunglasses on. There was an awkward silence as we decided what to do with our time together that day.

When Gary began speaking, I was reminded of the film *Nine and a Half Weeks*, and I started looking around for the hidden camera. He impressed me with his obvious ability to take complete control of a situation and capture my attention in full. Every detail spoke volumes. His perfect nose. His dark eyebrows. The way he walked. Was this his front or his true self, or did he even have a true self? As VP of marketing for his company, he had already admitted outright that he was an actor and that I was, too, in my illustrious occupation.

But throughout the time we were together, the question of which self he was displaying stayed uppermost in my mind. Was he acting how he thought I expected him to act? Or how he wanted to appear? Was this an act he maintained all the time? Was he constantly trying to live up to his own image of himself?

Perhaps he was wondering the same about me, but I must have come across as a bit more of an open book, as usual. His tone of voice dripped with sex. *He's just trying to create some sort of sexual intrigue*, I thought. His act was more for himself than for me. But it was working on me too…

25. NATURE

Gary had worked in film production in New York City for seven years and *had connections*. Apparently, this was something he deemed extremely important, as he made sure to emphasize it repeatedly, which made me think I had been missing the boat all along, in that I had no such *connections.* He hooked me up with a great photographer and helped me pick out the best shots to use. These shots came to be dubbed "the mom-of-the-nineties" headshots by a few casting directors. I had started making inroads and going out on commercial auditions, and he was fairly supportive and even wanted me to present myself professionally in pantsuits and such. I wanted to keep showing off my legs, however. I had to be contrary.

At his beach house, he revealed to me that, in addition to his townhouse in Beverly Hills, he had a house in New Orleans, a house in Sedona, Arizona, and an apartment in New York City—all as gifts from his parents. Then he complained about women using him for his money and connections. Poor baby. So why did he start out by telling me all about it? And what did I bring to the beach house? I despised the fact that my sexuality, looks, and personality were my only real bargaining chips. Did anyone in LA care about character? Integrity? Education? Could an exotic dancer even be seen as someone who has these qualities?

I didn't run in his circle; I hadn't been socialized with the upper crust, the jet set, the wheelers and dealers. I was just a small-town farm girl with big dreams who was still trying to make them come together at the ripe age of thirty. He was a financially successful, big-city guy with plenty of strings to pull. And, of course, he had to be extremely handsome. But that first night at the beach house, we simply sat in lounge chairs and stared out at the ocean. Then he walked me back to my beater car, and I drove home.

A few days later, he called me. We talked almost an hour, and by that point, I was sweating. It was dangerous to talk to him for so long—that almost equaled a third date. After I described how I liked getting onstage and teasing the idiots at the bar, he said, "I want you to tease me for an hour before we make love." Later he asked, "Are you 'working' me?" Maybe, maybe not. I really didn't know anymore. It was second nature. What did he really mean by "working"? Had he dated a dancer before? Could I believe anything he said?

Breathing deep, I tried to keep hold of myself to keep him from knowing that he had gotten to me. It was just a game of cat and mouse. But who was really the cat? Turn the tables, and it's a whole new game. I loved the provocative intrigue that led up to an initial sexual encounter, but I ultimately preferred sex in the context of a loving, committed, monogamous relationship, and that meant getting a blood test—together. How boring and anti-climactic, but otherwise there would always be a barrier between us.

Gary explained that it was hard for him to find a woman who could keep up with him and was beautiful as well. Pardon me, but my quest for Mr. Right was far more difficult than his quest for Mrs. Right, because as we all know, women are higher on the evolutionary scale.

My enchantment with a man always happened overnight. I would go from one extreme to another. I would become obsessed and lose all self-control. Then after he was gone, I would agonize and grieve, but ultimately, I would arrive again at the realization that success is the best revenge. So I would throw myself back into my work, proceeding to neglect my love life and eventually a raging desire for a man would build up again…and so on and so forth.

Why did I always feel like I was on the short end of the rope when I made love? Why did I always feel exploited even if I truly enjoyed the interlude? There was something lacking, I wanted some kind of supernova of psycho-spiritual-sexual bonding to take place. Orgasm! Yes, that's what was missing. But is that an emotional experience or just a sexual one? And can anyone really draw a line between the two? There was no way any man could ever completely understand me, yet still I harbored fantasies about that kind of transcendence on his part. He's only a man after all, not some omniscient being.

At his place in Beverly Hills, he ever so nonchalantly pulled open a desk drawer, found a small vial of cocaine, and mumbled, "Hmm, some more snuff. I forgot I had this. I'll have to introduce you to it sometime." He loved playing the big bad wolf, especially around me, Little Miss Wide-Eyed-Backwoods-Green-Around-the-Gills. He seemed to think that not only did the world revolve around him, he also dictated its RPM.

I was attracted to his wealth of knowledge and background, and to his mental sharpness and speed. But I would not be made to feel that I was supposed to be so indebted to his granting me audience that I had to keep my mouth shut and just listen to his advice from On High. If he didn't feel that my point of view was just as valuable as his, then I had run headlong right back into my recurring problem with men: their ego. As far as I could tell, if I wasn't running with the wolves, I was butting heads with the rams, or swimming with the sharks.

He said he wanted kids. He told me he had ended an engagement because they disagreed over how to raise kids. How tedious to have to explain my reasoning on the tiresome topic of reproduction again. Even if the argument of overpopulation and pollution wasn't convincing enough; most people's kids just become part of a herd of mindless sheep anyway, and where is the value in that? As if *his* kids would be *more special* than all the others. He wanted kids; he was a conformist.

My parents conformed too because they had kids. At least one of their kids became a true nonconformist. Dad said he had them because "It's just the thing to do. Everybody has kids." And he called himself a nonconformist. No, not everybody has kids. Is having kids about accepting your own mortality? Or is it perceived as some way to get a lock on immortality? Or is it a way to create people you can control and who will (hopefully) love you no matter what? It still seems to me that most people view them as a replacement model and then attempt to mold them into their own image, which completely robs the new people of their own individuality. Not my idea of quality time, on either side of that equation.

It came down to control, I suppose. My writing and my body were the things I could control (I thought), as opposed to other people, and it would be maddening not to be able to control my own child. So being alone always seemed more tolerable than enduring the endless frustration of dealing with outside entities who had other agendas. No matter what, it would always allow too much undue influence into my brain, which just wanted to see the world clearly.

My mother was getting worried about my not settling down and making babies, as I was getting close to the end of my twenties. I had already passed on a few chances, and my youngest brother was about to become a father. So I had to try to explain myself to her. First off, I had to be married in order to have a kid, and that was proving to be a challenge.

I didn't want my sexuality to just morph into the burden of raising children, certainly not by myself. I just could not figure out how that would fit into my spirited lifestyle without making me want to run screaming from the building. A woman's energy does emanate, in part, from her sexuality, and all women channel their sexual energy into some purpose or another. I wanted to keep my options open for as long as possible.

Up until then, I'd never found a man who was truly handsome, successful, educated, cultured, rich, and had a sense of humor. How could I expect Gary *not* to have an ego? I certainly had one. In spite of my need to be free and independent, I still felt a yearning for a man and still wanted the added protection and provision, but not the domination and control that men tend to expect or desire.

Why fight nature? I knew it would happen. We were two sexually charged creatures. The power of my sex drive hit me like a freight train. It was a herd of wild horses—untamed and uncontrollable. It had to be harnessed and channeled, turned into an asset and not a liability.

The guy had everything going for him and he was interested in *me*, so I immediately started to think something must be *wrong*. And the morning after, I found out what it was.

"So how do you feel about last night? Did you know you left scratches?" He showed me the scratches I had left on his back. I was speechless. I did that? I could not remember doing that.

Slowly, I got ready to leave, and he did not say anything about getting together again, so I asked if we could plan on next Wednesday. He said "Yeah sure, that's fine, but look, just don't get too attached to me." Smile. What? Round one: Gary. He didn't call for three days and so finally I called and tried to get him to get the blood test and he balked, calling it an insult. As if I should just trust him implicitly. He never called again. Going "off" Gary was like going through withdrawal from heroin.

Sure, I could have gotten married in Michigan at twenty-three to Jim. I could have married Mike in Colorado at twenty-six. I could have gotten engaged by that time in California, if that had been my focus. Obviously it wasn't. I'd made very little effort in the direction of finding suitable husband material. I simply stumbled onto a few opportunities, enjoyed them for what they were worth, and then they dwindled away for one reason or another. I was busy. I was trying to build a career. Really.

Was it my fault that all the men turned out to be assholes? It's not like they had a label on their heads. Wait, wait, so it's *my* fault for *choosing* assholes, but it's not their fault for *being* assholes? And why are there *so many* of them? Is there a problem in the parenting pipeline? Someone is not teaching boys to be sensitive, respectful of women, and compassionate.

Falling in love with a man meant ripping myself apart, my skin peeling off, taking off my clothes, pulling back the covers, and lying down in scalding water. Was I a masochist? Emotionally needy? Just plain crazy? We all know how it will end: pain and tragedy. Why keep pursuing those ends?

26. DUST, SUNSHINE, AND SCIENTOLOGY

In June of 1995, I flew home to celebrate the birth of my first niece. My brother's kids would be a magnet that would keep drawing me back home over and over until they left the farm, as I hoped they would someday. But they too would return, like homing pigeons. As I gazed out the window at the barnyard, I felt a strange commingling of the past, present, and future, like a watercolor painting, everything merging, swirling, and breathing together in a space above time. My parents' home was a sweet, innocent, old-fashioned world. The LA lifestyle I had been leading was cold, harsh, and edgy.

I had some money, which afforded me options, but what options were these? Travel? How could travel change anything? It could only change the context in which I saw myself on this planet, alter my perspective perhaps, but my basic identity would remain the same. I was still just an innocent farm girl kicking up dust on the country trails and dreaming of the heights to which she would rise while gazing up at the clear blue sky.

Back in LA, while my "mom-of-the-nineties" headshots were making their way around Hollywood, I stumbled across a soft-core porn opportunity. I had done some commercial auditions but had not booked anything at that point, and the extra money would come in handy. The producer was a woman who dealt only with natural women, and that was the deciding factor in my getting involved. I found it rather empowering: the perfect choice for a feminist actress looking for a few extra bucks without compromising herself with a hard-core situation.

The work was shot in Canoga Park in a huge house with a pool, like most porn shoots in LA. She loaned me a few pieces of jewelry, since I had none of my own. There was a tasteful segment in the huge bathroom with me in my long, black, lace gown. Then there was the pool sequence with me in a hot-pink suit that highlighted the important body parts. The sun glinted off my shoulders and earrings as she coached me in the appropriate facial expressions. It was one of those fleeting experiences that only become recognized as a high point much later in life.

Only a few dog-eared photos, hidden in my filing cabinet, remain to remind me of these gleaming moments under the Southern California sun. I never felt I compromised myself at all with that shoot.

For a so-called feminist to do work such as that is not at all hypocritical. Female good looks are, after all, a commodity highly sought after and commercialized, so why shouldn't a woman capitalize on her assets? Where the problem comes in is when others cannot see beyond this aspect of a woman, when she is judged and dismissed for turning her good looks into economic opportunity, or when she gets tunnel vision and sees only this aspect of herself as being viable at all.

No woman can get through Hollywood without a bout with a Scientologist, a Tom Cruise wannabe, a racecar driver, or a Porsche freak. Luckily I found all these in one man, so I saved some time. When you're that shallow, it's not hard to be full of yourself. Predictably, I met him at the club as well. He did his best to impress—and indoctrinate. He took me to the Scientology "Celebrity Centre" in Hollywood. Beautiful place, and it even had acting seminars and workshops. But as I relaxed in the ostentatious lobby, the feeling washed over me that this was just another cult, and I had to be careful not to get sucked into it. His bachelor pad was in Marina del Rey, and we got to know each other better there. But I do not believe he ever gave me his real name, just his "stage name" or racing name. Whatever.

He never really showed any interest in who I was or what I was about, and whenever I wanted to understand more about him, I was directed elsewhere—to L. Ron Hubbard. He felt I should be impressed enough with that and with his car. Of course he too was critical of me, telling me to just get the boobs, the nails, and the hair done in order to be a professional actress. Superficial, fake Hollywood. He told me to assert myself, take care of my image, and stop being such a hermit and a miser. OK, I'll work on it.

Why would any man care to look beyond a woman's beauty? Because she's beautiful. That typifies Hollywood's attitude toward women. The industry treats women as packages lined up on a shelf. Only the pretty ones get picked, according to their expiration date, only to have their insides scraped out with a spatula. American women are "classed" according to their looks. A guy in a bar once told me the only difference between a wife and a prostitute is the length of time involved. So I had to separate mind and body to keep my sanity in that sort of crass environment. But I felt so vacant and shallow about it that I knew I could not keep it up for long.

So I was starting to get it: Any woman who comes to LA alone, looking to be an actress, with no money, no connections, and no marketable skills, ends up having to dance in a bar to make the high rent and pay for pictures, classes, makeup, skincare, clothes, gym memberships, insurance, hair stuff, and on and on. Then she starts going off the deep end because things aren't opening up very quickly, and she gets involved in toxic relationships and drugs. She winds up on the streets in a few years because she loses all her focus and self-awareness due to the distractions, disappointments, and predators inherent in big-city life.

Did the entertainment industry want people like me? Intellectual and analytical? Not really. On the other hand, it seemed I was too radical for the generally conservative education system. Forcing myself to fit into it was suffocating. I was in limbo between two worlds that were not quite right for me. It set the stage for a double life.

They say there's a place for everyone, but can everyone find their place? Speaking of places, by that point, I had found a little room in a Craftsman-style bungalow in Santa Monica. I needed to be closer to auditions and did not appreciate living with fleas in the carpet. The house held four other roommates. One was a model from Australia with long, flowing hair; one was a gay wanna-be composer who watched *Friends* constantly; one was a young female exchange student from Germany; and the other was a thirty-something woman who had transplanted from the East Coast and needed to "lower her overhead." After moving in with my meager belongings, I did a corpse pose on the blessed hardwood floor and thought I had "arrived."

Hollywood was fickle, and I figured if things didn't develop with the acting, I still had my writing, and I knew I could make a killing in the skin trade without anyone finding out. But there was a constant fear that the money would stop flowing. It wasn't even characteristic of me to have money, because I'd been taught that principles were more important than money, which I took to mean I would live in "voluntary poverty" my whole life.

Is it unscrupulous to dance topless to raise money to start a school? What about dancing just to make sure I didn't have to call home begging for money to support an endeavor they didn't support? Coming to Hollywood was my idea, and I had to foot the bill for it, literally. So I felt like I was getting away with murder by dancing half naked for tips and spending all the money. Guilt and fear are the basis of 90 percent of human behavior. The rest is based on lust.

27. ESCAPE

But I had just turned thirty, and I had to make a detailed inventory of what the hell I was doing with my life. I'd danced for over a year, and unless I switched clubs or states very soon *and* supplemented my income with *something* else, I was going to break down. Sure the money was good, but I needed to maintain my sanity and my health too. How could I keep working in a smoke-filled environment?

Emotionally, I would never view men the same way I did before I started dancing, even though I wasn't too keen on them before. I could gloat over the fact that I had taken thousands of dollars in aggregate out of their collective pocket and used it to my advantage. But I was getting increasingly sick of doing "business" with them, because they were simply not worth eye contact.

Nightmares ensued in which a man was on a search-and-destroy mission in which everything I loved was the target. He watched me carefully for clues and then systematically tortured me by slowly killing those things while they were still in my arms. These beloved beliefs, dreams, and ideas were symbolized by a cat and a baby. I woke up knowing why some people go into hiding from the rest of the human race and why I could not continue to leave myself open to the psychological abuse the industry as a whole heaped on actors. I had to batten down the hatches of my soul to survive LA, but we learn by doing what we have to do.

Immediately following my thirtieth birthday, I was flat on my back at UCLA emergency, writhing in agony from a pelvic infection. That was when I decided it was absolutely time to take a break from Hollywood. Two months later, in mid-January, I packed the beat-up Corolla and bid everyone in the Santa Monica bungalow good-bye. I wondered aloud about whether I should take a shower first, and my German roommate said, "You're an adventuress now. Who cares about showers?" I grinned at her, hopped in the beater, and backed out of the driveway of the humble abode, where only six months earlier I had laid on the floor of that tiny room and thought I had arrived.

The sunset mixed with smog looked like hell chasing me as I drove east. Around Needles, I could finally see the stars again and breathe the cool, clean night air. I had escaped—just barely, but I was free again. I was headed to Colorado.

Jake was OK with me spending a few nights on my way through, but he had some sort of legal hassles to iron out and he didn't smile much while I was there. I was more of a nuisance than anything else. I called my dad, who was doing taxes. He didn't ask me about mine. I knew it would probably feel regressive, but returning home would take me back to the bare bones of my beginnings. Perspective was the one thing that LA did give me.

There was no sex with Jake; it just didn't interest me. His sexual attitudes and practices left much to be desired anyway. Perhaps I had used sex as a control mechanism or as a substitute for home ever since I left Michigan. No matter. I just wanted to watch the birds, write, and breathe the mountain air. Feeling such aching relief to be out of that place, I wanted to stay up on the mountaintop forever. The sky was lovely, clear, and sweet, but I had promises to keep and miles to go without any sleep.

As Jake worked or slept, I wrote, thriving in seclusion. Again I contemplated the idea of having children and came to the conclusion that no man these days would stick around for a fat chick and a screaming baby, and how could I sustain such a burden alone? Single motherhood was not a concept I relished, and I still maintained the conservative idea that all kids need a two-parent household, if at all possible.

Having ripped off the noose of the G-string, I laid into the chocolate and peanut butter. It was winter after all, and I just didn't give a shit about trying to look like a Victoria's Secret model anymore. I wanted to be healthy, free, and strong—not owned by a man, an institution, or my parents. I'd been trying to find the freedom I'd had on the farm in the "outside" world, but I realized that sort of freedom couldn't possibly be found anywhere else.

Back home, I went into exile. But I also looked at Michigan as if seeing it for the first time and I suddenly realized how far off the beaten path it really was, like a Canadian peninsula. I liked being away from it all, but I wondered how I could ever be there and not feel like I'd been let off the hook. Since I didn't have to interact with anyone and could go for weeks without even seeing anyone, I didn't have to worry about my appearance.

I was upstaged by trees, after all.

I lived without addictions. There was no TV or radio constantly blaring. There was no using food as a drug. There were no anxiety attacks over sex or relationships. I didn't even talk to my family much, except when my dad and I argued at three in the morning. I even went to church and sang in the choir, for lack of nothing else to do and to make my mother happy. I heard Dad mumbling something about "making up for her life of sin in LA."

I wondered what they really thought.

28. MUTINY OF THE BODY

"You're only a socially acceptable, desirable woman if you look like *this*" is the underlying message of every media image of women. Acceptable and desirable to whom? Even the skinny women who think they are up to snuff by the popular culture's standards snub a woman who doesn't appear, at first glance, to measure up as well. Thus my quest to attain the "bod of the moment" was really a thinly disguised attempt to appear to be socially acceptable to the upper crust. Until I attained this goal, my friends would all be fatter or older than me. So according to these standards, I was a complete failure. I was over thirty, fat, had no husband, no children, no savings, no house of my own, and no salary. But I think I always knew I'd end up like that, because it's the only way to be free.

Three months after returning home, my lower parts sent some strongly worded messages to me again and I went in for an ultrasound. I was told my right ovary was "bad" and had to come out. Not being ready to have someone take a piece of me, and having no health insurance at the time, I waited around and thought about getting a second opinion like my dad suggested.

A month later, I was doubled over in absolute agony and had to go in for emergency surgery. The ovary had ruptured. OK, so my body was confirming the fact that my mind honestly did not really want to spawn a child. Of course, mind and body are one and the same. It stood to reason that if I didn't make motherhood a priority, it wouldn't happen. Still, it seemed strange, like something was constantly being postponed.

The surgery revealed that my right ovary had become a low-grade granulosa cell tumor—nonaggressive, the surgeon said. Something nonaggressive—in *me*? All I heard at the time was "low-grade blah blah blah." So I didn't take it that seriously, but given the nature of the episode and the leftover ovary, I questioned her.

"Why didn't you just take both ovaries if the cells spilled out?"

"The other ovary is fine, and you're young. You can still have children."

"No, I don't think I will. I can't even manage my own life, let alone somebody else's."

She laughed. "Oh, you'll be fine. Go make babies," she instructed me in that lyrical way of hers.

I later realized that if she had taken everything I would have been shunted into menopause at the ripe age of thirty.

The chaplain at the hospital patiently listened to my whole story about how I felt I had cut myself off from my family forever by dancing in the club and then lying to them about it, and how I felt that maybe this was a punishment of some sort. She thought I didn't need to tell them; it was over and done, and the present was all that mattered. And she assured me that the cancer was not my fault. My nightmares at the hospital still involved some man obstructing my path.

As I recovered from yet another near-death experience, I took over the upstairs of my parents' farmhouse, baked bread, tended the farm market, cleaned the house, and walked the dog through acres of woods. What a life! Eventually I was able to go back to school to finish the teaching certificate that I had left unfinished in Colorado. It was quite a shift from my life as an independent single woman in Santa Monica with a commercial agent in Beverly Hills, dancing three nights a week, making $3000 a month, and studying screenwriting at UCLA. It became hard to review anything I wrote in LA, and it was even harder to believe that the person I was on the farm was the same person as the one who went to LA and did all that. How can someone transform so completely in the space of a month?

The drive to get around the next curve had been subdued, as I realized I couldn't take on the world like

I always thought I had to. I was literally burning out my female "balls." My idea of "world" had to change; it had to become more bite-sized and easier to digest. Everything had finally caught up with me. I had thought that since I followed a low-fat, high-fiber diet, and worked out a lot, I would be invincible, could push myself to the extreme, stress about everything, live up to impossible standards, and endure a string of unfulfilling relationships. I mean, there's a supplement to fix that, right?

Was this why I was thinking about death so much? Was I waiting for some "sign" that I was not going to die soon, that I would have at least another thirty years? I had forced myself to believe that I had to meet the standards of Hollywood and of all the jerks out there, because I thought if I didn't, I would not make any money or have any man or career at all. The jerks were cute, they had money, they knew people. In LA, that makes up for all character flaws.

My mother reached for a fork in the drawer, pulled out a small one, and said, "Baby fork. Don't like it." So I grabbed it and threw it onto the floor in a mechanical manner. She started laughing, and I went and stomped on it, then picked it up and bent it in half. We were laughing hysterically. It was our reaction to Dad's inability to get rid of anything without making absolutely sure (over a lifetime) that there was no possible use for it. It was as if he thought he'd be struck down by lightening if he threw something away. True, there's no such place as "away," but couldn't some things at least be away from the house? I guess I was there to help him begin to do that. I finally felt somewhat indispensable. Or maybe they were just taking advantage of me.

Dad told me that my whole goal in life should've been to find a mate, that everything else was a waste of time. He was so far off base about me and modern society with his claustrophobic, archaic attitudes that he sucked the oxygen right out of the room the minute he opened his mouth. I was happy with everything I'd done and I had virtually no regrets, but he didn't care about that. It wasn't about me being happy or free to be myself; I was just supposed to make some idiot *man* happy, primarily by talking to him like a child and acting like one half the time.

The irony is if a man wants marriage, chances are he's not that dynamic and probably not very good in bed. He can't get a woman into bed whenever he wants, so he decides he's got to rope one of them into marriage. A man who has a ton of charisma, sex appeal, brains, wit, looks, and money can have any woman he wants whenever he wants, so why should he get married? But that was the only kind of guy I wanted to marry. I wanted my ideal or nothing. Anything less was just a flimsy substitute for the stylish and substantial man who was taking his time showing up. He must have been busy. Like me.

Sure, sometimes I just wanted sex—until I finally got it, after going without it for many moons, just to have someone chase away the loneliness, if only for a brief interlude. And yet I was always left feeling even lonelier in the aftermath. But I did it again eventually.

Why can't love just be something I can just go pick up at the drug store? It is a drug after all, right?

I often went so long without sex that I got to the point where I just wanted to jump into bed with the next halfway decent man I encountered. Even these being few and far between, a great deal of dry time would go by. Not that life is supposed to be a bowl full of—you know, *cherries*—but cherries are a very succulent fruit. Perhaps I should write erotica. It's the next best thing to being there. I must absolutely start reading it. And while I'm at it, perhaps I'll watch some of dad's old X-rated videos...Oh, let's not go there, shall we?

On certain nights, I would stand in the driveway outside the sixty-plus-year-old farmhouse and just gaze at that patched-up work in progress. Part of the siding was a checkered mosaic of coverings my father had cobbled together during different phases of his life in that house. Every addition of sorts reflected his mood at the time. A tiny bit of light was always shining from my bedroom upstairs, until the wee hours of the morning. A dangling mobile of embedded leaves my mother had made hung outside the door, and it would make a clattering sound in the wind. The whole house was not actually visible due to the trees and all manner of vegetation surrounding it. And I would think, *Yeah, there's a story here*.

But if everyone writes a book, who would have time to read any of them? Most people are sucked into TV. Not me, however, I never owned one. The TV just sits there mocking you with its ease of operation: "C'mon, just the touch of a button and you'll be whisked away to la-la land, where the bills fade away and you can live that vicarious life you've been fantasizing about." What kills me is that this really *is* how so many "days of our lives" get wasted.

29. RED FLAGS

He was leafing through an upscale magazine when I arrived at my seat near the back of the plane. His arms were chiseled.

I was returning from a visit to Boulder to see my old buddy Jake. I settled into my seat and struck up a conversation with the man with the arms. His name was Larry, and at thirty-five, he was just finishing chiropractic school in Chicago. His parents had divorced when he was in preschool. Red flag. His mother was an alcoholic. Another red flag. He was an only child. Third red flag. He had been in one relationship after another ever since high school and his idol was Elvis. Blazing red flags. He was getting ready to move to Atlanta in three weeks. Perfect. I introduced him to my parents after we got off the plane in South Bend, Indiana.

Over dinner on the second date, he asked me what I was looking for in a man. "Intelligence," I stated, without hesitation. He told me he was looking for someone "beautiful and teachable." Later I found out that I was the oldest woman he had ever gone out with. So he wanted someone he could train to be his little slave. How refreshing. Yet another man who had been brainwashed by the American mentality that a young beautiful wife boosts a man's status.

After telling him about my schooling, money problems, and trying to find a job, he wondered why a woman would work if she didn't have to. "Why didn't you just find a man?" he asked. "Work really doesn't do anything for you, except make money. If you already have a source, what's the point?"

Out of the blue, he described his time in a nude club in Atlanta that his "buddy" had "dragged" him to last year.

I held off on revealing the fact that I had been a dancer.

I wanted to see what he would reveal to me without that bit of information. Surprisingly, the man could easily talk about more cerebral and spiritual subjects, which floored me, since I didn't expect him to be able to carry on a conversation at all. He actually had a sense of humor, and we carried on a goofy repartee between the more serious subjects.

We went Christmas shopping in Michigan City, and I was sort of bored with shopping and beating around the bush.

"There must be a lot of beautiful women in Atlanta since that's what you said you looked for in a woman."

"Yeah, there are actually. When I saw the women there, I definitely left with a good impression of Atlanta."

"But those women may not actually live in Atlanta. They could be living anywhere."

"I talked to one dancer who had just bought a $200,000 house in Atlanta."

"Well, I suppose some of them might go ahead and buy a house. They do make good money, I've heard."

We went into the Eddie Bauer outlet and I browsed as he stood next to me. His scent invaded my brain. I stuttered.

"Y-You know, I was—a, um…"

"What?"

"Oh, nothing."

He shrugged and wandered away to another part of the store. A minute later, he came back, put his elbow on the clothes rack, and just stood there staring at me. I walked past him on my way to the counter with clothes over my arm. Unable to contain myself, I grinned at him like the Cheshire cat. And we both knew. So on the ride back to St. Joseph, I came unhinged.

"OK, the reason I'm interested in your perspective on the clubs and stuff…is because…when I lived in LA

I danced…a little."

"What? Really? Wait. I can't even picture you like that (he stared at me while driving). You're making that up."

"No, I'm not. I'd never lie about something like that. And, um, what do you mean you can't see me like that?"

"Well, I just never thought of you in that context. I've been kind of been avoiding the sexual side of you, since I'm moving. What did you wear?"

Preposterous. This is the first question they ask.

"What do you think I wore?"

"I'm just trying to get a mental picture."

"Does this somehow change how you see me?"

"Well, yeah. It makes me want to have sex with you."

I snapped my head to look at him. "Why does it make such a difference? Are you telling me you never even considered it until now?"

"Well yeah, but I thought you didn't want to since I was leaving in three weeks, so I was avoiding thinking about you that way."

"Maybe this has something to do with the fact that I'm peaking sexually, while you—being a man—are way past your peak. I was considering not seeing you anymore because I am attracted to you and I know you're leaving. (sigh) So there's a big conflict going on here. I haven't had sex in a year."

"*A year?*"

"Yep. And I'm sitting here thinking I should just assume that you are not desperate, that you probably had sex last weekend. There must be some discrepancy between our sex lives due to the fact that you're a man and I'm a woman."

I stared out the window while I unloaded all of this—afraid to look at him. Then I kicked myself for having unloaded. That always backfires. Nobody is ever ready for all that luggage to come crashing down.

"No, I didn't have sex last weekend. It's been…around two months. But I was thinking that perhaps this time—if it was going to happen—it could, because we have the office. So I came prepared."

"You've got condoms?"

"Yeah." He grinned at me.

I found that a little presumptuous, but it confirmed that he was indeed attracted to me, even though there was never much question of that. And with so much out in the open, the adrenaline kicked in. There was no way it wasn't going to happen now. I had to explain my process of justification to him.

"I remember you did ask me about my views on sex the first time we went out. And I said that sex without love left me feeling emptier than before. So what I usually do is fall in love *while* I'm having sex."

We laughed.

We went to his friend's office, but the door was locked and he didn't have a key. It was usually unlocked, or so he said. We got back into the van, and I didn't know what to do.

"Well, maybe this wasn't a good idea after all," I said. "Maybe I should go."

"No, I don't think so."

He leaned over, lifted up the arm on the seat, and kissed me. And did not stop kissing me. The temperature went through the roof as I returned the pressure of his lips. His tongue went through my body as I squirmed to get as close to him as possible, even though we were kissing across the ravine of the stick shift. Then he reached down and pulled the seat release, and I found myself in a lovely reclined position. He crawled over and settled his solid body over me. I felt so incredibly shielded and safe from the whole world—like a war could break out around us at that moment and we would both emerge unscathed.

After a few minutes of this heaven, he stopped and murmured in my ear, "I think we should get a room."

Something in me heard this as a statement of wanting a relationship. But that's not what he meant. Always take a man's words at face value, especially when it comes to sex.

"Really?"

"Yeah, I want to relax with you. I don't want to be in some car."

We got a room at the Marriott with a separate, spacious hot tub. He must have felt sorry for me and really wanted this to be special—even if it was only one night.

I freshened up in the huge bathroom. I took off my jeans and my granny underwear, as I really had not expected this to happen. After I cleansed, I modestly put the black jeans back on, sans underwear. They were the same jeans I had worn on the plane when I met him. Well, they did something for my rear end. I had on a pink satin T-shirt under a black sweater that zipped up the front, so it appeared I did want to at least drop a hint that day.

He looked up as I emerged from the bathroom, and he seemed surprised. Did he expect me to be naked? I expect a real man to execute my disrobing. He had started the water running and had discarded one of his shirts. We snuggled next to each other on the bed while the water ran and then I asked him to turn off a light. He got up and did as I asked. When he came back to me, I absorbed him at the edge of the mattress. We devoured each other on our knees, and I tore off my black sweater. I reached under his shirt to feel his muscles. Then he lifted my pink shirt over my head, unhooked my front clasp bra, and took one whole areola into his mouth. My body dematerialized into molecules moving so fast that I was no longer a solid object.

30. DROPPED OFF

The next day I woke up feeling alive again. At that moment, I knew I had to have a man in my life. I couldn't be that militant of a feminist or that isolated of an artist to cut off all chance of being able to have a love life and a sex life. I wasn't a sex addict; I just couldn't expect the cerebral to fill the void in me that wanted the visceral.

We had sex six times one night—at the office, after I dressed up for him (yes, I had held on to my "alternative lifestyle" wardrobe). Ten years later, that record still stood. He told me his record was twelve. I had never been with a guy who could go more than just one round.

Sex does "nail" you quite literally to the present moment. If you are fully engaged in the act, there is no way you can worry about tomorrow or brood about the past. It's just two people in the moment, merged with each other, moving and breathing together, both focusing completely on the act, on their sensations, and hopefully on each other. What is better than that? All the senses are alive and humming synergistically.

My problem was some anxieties were not completely obliterated from my mind. They still retained the outer edges of my consciousness, doing play-by-play analysis: Does my vocalization do anything for him? Should I fake it? Am I doing this right? How long will he stay down there? Will he expect that much from me? But I get tired and it gags me. I just have to work on it longer. Is he going to come soon? He probably thinks I'm fat.

Then when I did get "serious" with a man, I immediately wanted to figure out "where this is going." It was like constantly riding in the passenger's seat. I never came to pick him up, and we never went to my place because I never seemed to have a place of my *own*, with no roommates. I was finally tired of living in limbo.

However, after seeing him a few more times, I had to take a good hard look at what I had actually snagged off the plane: he idolized a dead rock star, had an adulterous best friend, talked about polygamy as if it were a legitimate lifestyle choice, got high on nitrous oxide among other things during his lackluster twenties, wanted to read *Mein Kampf*, pretended to be educated, dressed as if he already had money, and was only going into chiropractic for the money. *And* he had the nerve to talk about "Sunset's" lewd antics at the nude club during dinner with me. Who says I wasn't selective?

On the other hand, even if I never saw the guy again after he moved, it was fantastic for three weeks. Three weeks—even three hours—was better than nothing. It was good that we would be separated for a while right after getting to the sex stage. I figured it would give us time to discover how we really felt in the absence of each other. Perhaps he wanted to prowl around Atlanta and see who was available—some gorgeous dancer, perhaps. Maybe he had a woman waiting for him. He reeled me in; he could probably reel any woman in. Then again, I was desperate.

I felt I just wasn't pretty enough or rich enough or socially acceptable enough to get the man I really wanted. Most men wanted a wife who conformed to certain social standards, and I had to acknowledge that I was somewhat eccentric. Wanting to be married was not going to make the right man walk into my life and marry me, and since I couldn't control that, I decided I'd rather not deal with it at all. Erasing the whole episode from my memory seemed the best way to go. I wanted the sex and I got the sex, so that was the end of it. At least I knew that I was still capable of getting sex, so that boosted my sexual confidence.

I could feel like a real woman again.

Once again, however, I was uncapped. Overnight my emotional well-being had again been turned over to a man. My entire mood was controlled by whether or not he called. I despised myself like that. All I could do was try to distract myself with studying. But attempting to concentrate on anything else was like collecting feathers in a windstorm.

Fresh off this affair, I began my student teaching at the high school from which I graduated, fantasizing about reliving my high school days, only as a liberated, somewhat aroused thirty-year old teacher, not as a repressed farm girl. But my attraction to a few of the seniors was jarring, as I sat in front of the class with a visualization of that unforgettable description of the acrobatics of a certain nude dancer floating through my mind. He told me she had done a handstand between his legs, balancing her legs on his shoulders. Then I wondered if the cute guy in class had been with very many women. How did he kiss? How long could he go? How many times in one night? Maybe a younger guy would do me some good. I thought I'd just wait for them to graduate and then do some exploring. Maybe one of them would like to go back to LA with me. *I was crazy.*

I finally reeled myself back in by reminding myself that they probably had girlfriends. On the other hand, maybe they fantasized about me. One of them always acknowledged me in the hall and made quite mature contributions in the classroom. Like I said, concentration was quite beyond me at the time.

He had gone back to Atlanta and had not left me a number, but I had to reach him, so I decided to try the number I got from directory assistance. The first two times I tried, I got a woman's answering machine, which said, "I'm not here right now. Leave a message." Bravely and foolishly, I kept trying.

Finally someone answered—a woman. I stuttered, "Oh, uh, I'm looking for a Larry Smith. I'm calling long distance."

"Oh yes, he's right here. Honey, it's for you."

Honey. My pelvis went down a laundry chute. He was *married?! No*, he couldn't be. He had already *met* someone else? He had moved in with another woman? Why did I think he didn't have a girlfriend?

"Hello?"

"Larry? It's Mandy."

"Oh hey, can I call you back? I just got out of the shower. Are you at home? Will you be there all day?"

"Yeah, it's a snow day."

"What?"

"There's no school; we're snowed in."

"Oh, OK. I'll call you back, OK?"

"OK."

Click.

31. CLOSURE

With men, their jokes are their truth, hidden within the punch line. But the former isn't funny and the latter isn't true. I pity men. But that doesn't mean I'm not mad as hell at them. I could not believe how low they could go. Larry was probably married—or pretending to be a polygamist. Why can't men just come out and say they're no good? Actually, most of the time they do, but women just hear what they want to hear.

Of course, I never heard from him again. Maybe he moved in with one of his girlfriends from Chicago. Maybe she was one of the strippers from Cheetah's who had bought the house he mentioned. He'd probably had sex with his best friend's wife too. And this was a clan from little old St. Joseph, Michigan. So much for the old-fashioned, traditional ways of life in small-town America.

Why did this surprise me? I'd lived in LA and I still thought there were decent human beings out there? How does one live in a world that completely lacks principles? My parents had not been out in the jungle. They couldn't be relied on for guidance of any sort. That's why I had to be a wolf—a predator. Kill or be killed. But even if I initiate it, I still feel like a man is stealing from me when he's having sex with me.

I can see life's tail lights
disappearing down the highway
leaving me far behind—
left alone
to deal with age.

Finishing my three months of student teaching was like digging ditches in the back forty. Just to get out of my parents' house again and to fill the void, I moved in with a cute, older special-ed teacher from Kalamazoo who fell hard for me. He was supportive of my writing, so he set up a little space for me and my computer. His kids were a nuisance, however.

The idea of dancing again wafted through my brain and it excited me, even if it would be partly due to economic necessity. I would just waltz back into the club and ask for my old schedule. They were cool to me there. I always got the days I wanted, the girls weren't all bitches, the sound and light systems were great, and even though the clientele wasn't exactly high class, they were fun and friendly. And it really was a safe club.

I still looked the same, I was almost finished with my certification, I had rested, and my credit cards were paid off. Why did I need a job by next fall? Maybe it would take me another year to find the right school. In the meantime, I could dance. No one ever needed to find out. No one ever had found out. I was tired of staying "undercover," so to speak, yet I didn't want to suffer from "overexposure" again. I just had to limit the time in the club, I figured, and balance it out with other aspects of my life.

It was increasingly apparent that the only time I felt really confident was when I was on the stage or on the page. I had no confidence in my ability to hold a job—any kind of a job. I had been "fired" from my first student-teaching debut, fired twice from hostessing, and fired from food service. So I had developed an insecurity complex about the work world. I could get up on a stage all by myself and do anything from a comedy routine to singing a solo to modern dance improvisation to getting nearly naked, but I was petrified when it came to "working."

On March 27th, 1997, my dad called and told me to turn on the news. After that, I no longer had to wonder where Steve was. I had narrowly avoided being sucked into one of the most dangerous cults ever: Heaven's Gate.

He had said he was willing to die for the man. In the "farewell video," he looked so different—bloated and frozen—but I recognized those mannerisms, gestures, and vocal traits. He was trying so hard not to be himself. He was attempting to act "beyond human," but his fear still seeped out the edges. Everything came tumbling out of closets and attics I thought I had shut tight and locked.

If only I hadn't been so angry with him, I thought. I wouldn't let up on the interrogation about *her*. It drove him away. *Was it all my fault?* Perhaps he finally found out what the angels think, do, and prioritize. Or maybe he paid too high a price to get into their club.

I felt the need go to the press with my story. The man I knew was not a lunatic cultist. He was a brilliant, sensitive man. I had to try to let people know that anyone at all could be drawn into these strange groups, even a small-town girl from the Midwest. Especially a small-town girl from the Midwest. An image of me, wide-eyed and holding a picture of him, wound up on the front page of the *South Bend Tribune*. Never imagined that would make the front page.

I unearthed the book I had written about the whole episode with him and the cult, and decided it needed to become a screenplay, which turned into another decades-long project.

32. KICKBACK

Wonder of wonders, in August of 1997, I actually got a teaching position for 9th and 10th grade English in the small town where I had gone to Sunday school, for a stupendous salary of $27,000! At last I would be able to start building some sort of career, even if it was academic and low-paid. My dream at that point was just to get a decent car and get out of my parents' house again. But it would be a fate worse than death to get permanently stuck in that tiny rural town of eight thousand other stuck people. My brothers had never left, and it showed. Getting out of there would take money; staying out would take more money, as in a decent, secure income.

But after only two months of my first year teaching, I wanted to run screaming back to California. In October, a student had written me a note explaining that if I didn't deposit $10,000 in the back dumpster, he'd "rape my beautiful body till it was black and blue."The administration told me to "let it go."

For six long months I had to look out over all my students every day and wonder who the deranged individual was. Finally, in March, he handed in a handwritten assignment, the first assignment he had turned in that year. The content of this work was equally disturbing. I took the two handwriting samples down to the principal's office to compare, and it was a dead-on match. So at last the kid was called on the carpet, and I was told he started crying. He left my class before the end of the month.

Two of my students outdistanced their cohorts in making my life a living hell. The Top Dog Rebel kindly wrote me a note that explained, "You have absolutely no communication skills whatsoever, and you should crawl back under the rock you came from." It seems I wasn't able to teach him anything about dangling prepositions. After I foolishly telegraphed my horror and threw the note in the trash, another young starlet, ignoring my warnings, took it out of the wastebasket and proceeded to read it out loud to the class. She then skipped back to her seat as I squelched the impulse to squeeze the life out of her body like a boa constrictor.

Later on, Top Dog Rebel argued with the principal in the classroom about freedom of speech, and don't students have it in school? No, actually that freedom is not without restriction. The kid would make a great lawyer someday, I thought. That was my roughest class—the "regular" group. The "advanced" class was actually civilized. I may have gotten through to a couple of them.

In April, to top off the year, one girl asked me, in front of the class, "Did you have a boyfriend who was in the Heaven's Gate cult?" Being caught off-guard and thinking it was common knowledge anyway and that she already knew the answer, I said, "Yes." After all, it had been on the front page of the paper only a year ago. So later I was blamed for "telling them about the cult." In another unrelated incident, a fight almost broke out in my classroom, and that was the last straw for the administration. They decided to make me a permanent substitute at an elementary school just up the road from the farm. After speeding home crying in my mother's Volvo and getting a ticket to boot, I realized it was probably all for the best and would lower my stress level and my commute.

Then, like a blessing from On High, the non-smoking law was passed in California in 1997. Finally, I could make tax-free cash in a smoke-free environment. I had some money saved, a better car, and a teaching certificate. There was also my *extensive* previous experience in the industry: a Groundlings class, some commercial auditions, and the screenwriting class. That, combined with a hair-raising year of small-town teaching and dealing with my parents, was enough to make me think LA was worth another try.

So a few days after the end of the school year, I packed my "new" 1993 red Honda Civic hatchback and headed west again. There's a lot to be said for cruise control and air-conditioning.

I landed with a friend in Torrance and found a studio apartment near Culver City within two weeks of my return to the Golden State. Then I just glided into my old money-making hangout and everyone remembered me. It had only been a little over two years, after all. Wow.

Three weeks later, I was lined up with the other girls, preparing to do the obligatory "birthday dance," when I glanced over at the bar and noticed a rugged fellow with blue eyes standing there, just staring at me. As soon as I was freed up, I hustled over, smiled at him, asked his name, and asked if he wanted a dance, knowing what the answer would be. His name was Pete, and I was surprised by his polite and gentlemanly manner, since it was a working-class bar. There was also his voice. It was deep and measured, as if every word was carefully chosen.

He owned an auto shop across the street and said that the bar was like *Cheers* for him; everyone knew his name. He talked about his sons, since it was Father's Day, and he was clearly disappointed that he was not able to see them due to the rift from his divorce. He asked if I'd like to "grab a bite" sometime. I declined, but accepted his card later that night. Over the next three days, the thought of him kept pushing its way into my mind. And I anticipated seeing him again, even though I knew he wasn't part of my plan.

Pete was simple-minded, lacking higher education, but he was streetwise and clever, having grown up in Long Beach, California. The divorce had raked him over the coals financially and emotionally, like so many other men, and he was actually living at his auto shop. But within weeks, he was spending most nights with me on my futon in my studio apartment.

I was more relaxed than I'd ever been in LA. Rent was no problem, even at $600 a month. Besides that, all I had was a manageable car payment. Even working only three nights a week would yield that—easily. So I very slowly began to figure out what I was doing with this new man.

He was a romantic—even at forty-five. And he talked about love first, well before I mentioned the word. He was extremely handsome—a Chuck Norris with a mustache, but no beard. Yet he was so much more than that: protective, supportive, considerate, and kind. But how could he have seen me as marriage material? He came on like a fire truck and stuck like glue. Crazy glue.

I told him about my past—my pattern of short-term affairs. They—or I—left for parts unknown; things just changed. Perhaps I showed signs of not being in a position to be committed. I changed my mind at the drop of a hat; I was always talking about other options, other plans, other places. The concept of stability was lost on me. He definitely needed a woman in his life and didn't like being single; it does take a brave person these days to be an active single. So after using the French glove for quite some time, we went together for a blood test, and that's when I knew this man could be trusted. At least at that exact time.

A few weeks later, I had a horrible night at work. I could not concentrate because Pete was there for most of the time, and I could not deal with him even glancing at another woman. That was another reason I had such a problem with relationships. The mere passing thought that *my* man might think someone else was more attractive than me made me so enraged—not jealous of her, but angry at him. Did I even glance at other men outside the context of my service sector job? I could not care less about them beyond that. If I could, I'd take an assault weapon in there and annihilate every last one of them. What's so hard to understand about that? I don't look at men the way men look at women. That was why it threw me for a loop when I found myself attracted to Pete. How could I be attracted to the enemy?

33. MEN

In the summer of 1999, about a year after we met, we started looking for a condo to rent in Orange County. We found one just barely on the other side of the Orange Curtain, as the area is so lovingly referred to by those from LA County. It was in Seal Beach and only twenty minutes from work. We moved into a building that housed mainly seniors, sort of a pre-Leisure World. Boring, but quiet. Sterile, but clean. Pete joked that I would give all the old guys a heart attack.

Speaking of old guys, my parents told me they were going to attend a class reunion at Berkeley in May and were planning on taking a train cross country, and I thought that sounded wonderful. They rarely left the farm and they needed to get out.

I didn't want to get my nails done, yet I couldn't escape a sense of obligation because *Pete* liked it—both the look and the smell of new nail polish. I hated the smell. I had to remind myself that if he was attracted to me for my looks, he would be gone when my looks were gone. I was a second wind to him—an escape from midlife crisis, loneliness, and disappointment. I never got my nails done.

It was 4am and I couldn't sleep, and I didn't want to go to Nevada with him because I hated that state and I didn't want to learn how to gamble and I wanted that godforsaken screenplay to sell and I didn't know what I was doing anymore. A few production companies had read it, but it hadn't quite made it to the green-light district. But I figured Pete was worth staying with at least for the time being, and we had discussed getting married. Did I have anything better to do? What I needed, no one could give me. Just myself.

If the screenplay didn't sell, I just wanted to get out of the country. Teaching in America is hell; there is no respect for education here. The only reason to stay would be Pete, and he had to be an absolute magnet to keep me with him. I wanted to travel and teach in other countries when I got too old to dance.

But what if I couldn't find a teaching job and he expected me to quit dancing? I thought I could always sell my car to move to Europe. Los Angeles is the only place where a car is truly necessary. Then I could just live on a shoestring and figure out how to pay off my student loan teaching in France or Germany. Yes, always other places, other plans.

Trying out a wig at the club was my next big project. What an experience to have long hair to flaunt. But the guys could see the difference between my bangs and the wig, so I still had more to learn on the finer points of fake hair. All at once, the manager came up and told me I had a call on the pay phone. I knew it was Pete, but why would he try so hard to reach me at the club? He was right across the street, after all.

"Sweetheart, listen, your father had a heart attack on the train. They were in Elko, Nevada, but they're flying him to Salt Lake City. I went ahead and bought you a plane ticket, and it leaves tomorrow morning. I'm so sorry, honey."

The wig was ripped off before I got to the back room, shoes were thrown into the backpack, and the G-string went flying. With street clothes chasing after me, I ran out of the building like it was on fire.

Was this it? As I sped home, I considered the implications and found that I worried primarily about my mother. This was only heart attack number two, but it sounded major. At least I wasn't far away, and I could be with her through the ordeal.

On the plane, I was edgy. I grabbed a taxi to the hospital and raced up four flights of stairs to find Mom on the pay phone. I dropped everything and hugged her, gasping for breath as I struggled to keep from dissolving into a puddle of tears. She told me he had a small stroke on the helicopter, and his face looked different. Then she took me to his room. She went in first; I tiptoed in behind her.

His body was small and pale—vulnerable. Seeing all the IV tubes hooked up to him and the heart monitor and the electrodes pasted on his chest, something turned over in me. He was only human, after all. When I saw his face, I collapsed my head onto his chest in tears. With a sigh of relief, he said, "Oh, hi baby, thanks for coming." He put me to work getting him ice chips because his swallowing ability had been affected by the stroke and they thought he would choke on water. I was shaking as I fed him the ice, stunned that I felt the way I did. Here was my dad—the invincible, stubborn, cantankerous man I knew him to be—needing to be fed, reduced to a helpless state.

I thought I was more concerned about Mom, but that did not seem to be the case at all. I realized that I would go to the ends of the Earth for either of them.

The doctors said he'd be in the ICU for at least two days and that we should go find a place to stay in town. We found an apartment in a house that made us feel like we were college roommates. It was springtime, and we spent time together in a tulip-infested downtown Salt Lake. I believe my mother actually enjoyed herself.

Visiting Dad back at the hospital was not so enjoyable, however. Every time Mom and I left the hospital for more than two hours, he would complain about where we had been all that time. Within fifteen minutes of us showing up, he was ranting about his sister, the bank, and all the "cheaters" out there masquerading as organic, as I watched the monitor show his heart rate go up every time he raised his voice. I paced back and forth at the foot of his bed, seething with a blinding concoction of hatred, love, and rage that I wanted to unleash, but I could not do it in the ICU. Yet that was where everything bubbled to the surface and boiled over. It was just so quintessentially maddening to see him like that even at death's doorstep.

All sorts of specialists came in to see him: a neurosurgeon, endocrinologists, speech pathologists, ophthalmologists, and, of course, the cardiologist, who drew a picture of the three major arteries in his heart. It was based on the information they got from the hospital he was in for his first heart attack, ten years before. One artery was completely blocked, one was 60 percent choked off, and one was 30 to 50 percent clogged. But they would have to wait for the stroke to resolve and heal before they could do any major surgery. They told him that he had to get his diabetes under control since it was a major factor in his heart disease.

Later on, in rehab, he seemed to get quieter, but he still argued with the cardiac educator about meat. I watched him hold my mother and tell her they needed to go home and put his affairs in order. Mom still wanted to get to California; he could recover out there for a while, she said, instead of stressing out on the farm over the bank and insurance and all. But no, Dad wanted to go home. He was starting to realize that he may not have much time left and that the rest of his life was going to revolve around the management of his diseases. The doctors had told him he had six months to live unless he got a bypass, but he didn't want to get a bypass because it could trigger another stroke.

He had me come to his bedside and put the railing down so we could hug each other. Through the tears, he said he appreciated everything I was doing for Mom, and I told him I was sorry if I was mean while I was living with them. Then he told me, "I think you and Pete should go for it." And that's when I decided it was time to get married—before my father died.

34. IF THE SHOE FITS

So it became a push for marriage, not because of an imminent birth, but because of an imminent death. Heck, I worried about Pete's health too. His dad had died of a heart attack at forty-five and his brother had already had one; Pete was forty-seven. It was as if my life was finally beginning, and people around me were...Well, life is short, after all. When I finally took care of my own health and found a new gynecologist, I reported to her that the 1996 incident was "benign." Well, that was close enough to "low-grade," I thought. I hadn't even bothered to bring my medical records with me from Michigan to California.

What will I feel when I look back as I lay dying? Will anyone be there? Will I even want anybody there? Maybe I won't even know if anyone is there. And most importantly, will my life have been meaningful in some way? Who can answer these questions? What is truly meaningful anyway?

It was becoming clear that I would be drifting back and forth between Michigan and California indefinitely. Pete was fundamentally Southern California: cars, bars, and freeways. He was actually like a freeway: solid and straightforward. I had no reason to think that he hadn't been honest with me. I had met his family, but his divorce was still not final after almost three years. He often mumbled something about me getting tired of him and dumping him. Did he think I'd be better off with someone closer to my age?

Furthermore, I couldn't tell the truth to anyone—not about the dancing and certainly not about the fact that he wasn't even divorced yet. I was not the type of person who could just dance around the truth and never come out with it. But for the time being, I had to, as I was not yet a part of Pete's family. I had been in purgatory many times before, so who knew what would transpire? I had actually thought I might marry each of the previous men.

Some people may assume that anyone who isn't employed and married by the time they're in their thirties must be defective in some way. But I was not defective; I just maintained high standards at all costs. If anything or anyone was right for me, I figured it would just fit; no pushing or prodding would be needed on my part. Perhaps this sounds somewhat self-centered, but I see it as individualistic and libertarian. Isn't that the mark of a genius? Or just an ornery bitch who actually *is* defective in some way?

So many Type A males who are leaders in their field are absolutely unbending. Why should I be any different? If I were a man, I would be seen as ambitious and full of initiative, with exceptionally high standards. The world, by and large, still does not wish to give women their way, even if it is the better way. Too many men still cannot handle the idea that any woman may be smarter and/or stronger than they are; there is still too much male animosity and testosterone burning up the highways and setting up war zones.

My reaction to most problems was spending time alone. Pete's reaction was to be there for me. He had spent years solidifying habits that had to do with being part of a couple. I had spent years developing habits that revolved around being single. He was so much more familiar with domestic chores that he had to teach me the proper way to make a bed—with the corners tight.

"Don't you know how to make a bed?" he asked, exasperated.

"Why should I know how to do corners like that?"

"Because you're a *girl*."

"Oh, I see. So that's a *girl's* job. Well, I guess it's easier than learning to fix cars, but frankly, I think either sex can make a bed."

So, somewhat sexist attitudes emerged. And he wanted me to be an appendage in everything he did, but I wasn't sure I would be able to accommodate him every single time, nor would I want to. What about trips on my own? Part of me would always yearn to be completely independent. The part of me that wanted to merge with a man had been eroded by years of antagonism, disappointment, and anxiety, and it was just getting old like I was. But he was so commitment-oriented, so supportive, and so caring. If he could meet me halfway, and I could accommodate his plans most of the time, I thought we might be OK.

We went to Laughlin, Nevada, on a bowling trip, even though I was hot and uncomfortable most of the time. I went to the swap meet with him, and that also was too hot. When we were out with his family for his birthday, I had severe cramps and was flowing like the Mississippi. And I went to the party his old coworkers had for one of their buddies, even though I was uneasy, since I didn't know anyone. The truth is, it's very hard for a divorced man's new girlfriend to integrate with his family and friends. The family was raised by another woman, and the friends go way back. There's a whole history there of which I wasn't a part, so I would always feel like an outsider.

I still had the feeling that I was filling shoes, that I had been labeled in his mind as his "Significant Other" and that the person with that label needed to behave a certain way. He would introduce me to other men with a tone that was looking for approval, like "What do you think? Not bad, huh?" I told him how much I hated being referred to with pet names—as if I were a pet—and how much I hated being shown off or put on display just to make him look good. Like all the others, he too had been conditioned to see women as cheerleaders and domestic queens, but this time I tried to overlook it. I was in my mid-thirties after all and I truly did not want to spend the rest of my life alone.

It was clear that he felt like nothing without a woman. He told me his closest friends while growing up were female. The guys just beat up on him. He fought back and gained some respect, but gained the most from being popular with the girls—not because he was a "stud," but because he could win their sympathy. When his family bumped him around, he befriended the girl next door. When his marriage finally collapsed, he took up with another woman almost immediately. After they broke up, he spent more time at the club, where he met me. Then we became attached at the hip. It was a good thing he didn't have more time and money, or I would have had no time at all to myself.

Marriage notwithstanding, until I sold my writing, I felt that my only economic vein in society would draw on my looks. The real aptitudes and talents I had were apparently not truly valued. So I felt like some sort of paper doll, a wind-up toy, "put ten dollars in and I'll do a dance for you." But like someone once said, sometimes you have to crawl through the mud and walk over hot coals and stick needles in your eyes before you can pay someone your life savings to learn to fly. But then how can you fly with all that mud stuck between your fingers?

One day he actually told me, "I think you're going to wake up when you're forty years old and realize that you haven't done anything with your life." He thinks I just had "fun" for ten years? Sure, living on the edge on a shoestring is "fun." Feeling like an outsider is "fun." Being uncertain and unstable is "fun." The only time I was happy in Boulder was when I was hiking, biking, or dancing. Still "playing," I guess. But what is so wrong with that? What was I *supposed* to be doing, according to him? He didn't understand or value what I *had* done, because it didn't make money. And he did not have time to be concerned about the fact that some artists and some people can take a long time to find their niche in life. Some never find it.

American society is not exactly forgiving to those who don't fit in, who don't toe the line in a capitalist system. Is the family farm worth nothing because it doesn't turn a major profit? And Van Gogh's work was actually worthless until he died? Emily Dickinson's poems did not resonate until after she passed? All creative work is an act of blind faith.

Pete worked with the tangible, yet people came to him rather than to some other mechanic, because they liked him as a person. So he was actually selling something intangible: his character, his honesty, his reputation. And that was where his true value lay. It wasn't that the car or truck was fixed; it was that *he* fixed it, that people liked *him* and trusted *him* to do the work. Artists and thinkers "sell" ideas, words, emotions, stories, yet these are ultimately priceless. How can you price something that ultimately exists beyond the economic realm?

I had a hard time getting over the hurdle of one full year in the same place. After I decided (again) that I didn't want to act (in Hollywood) and ran out of possibilities for the screenplay, I set aside everything I came back to LA for and focused on getting a teaching job because I knew that:

A. The dancing wasn't really enough money
B. It couldn't last forever
C. It wasn't conducive to a relationship
D. Maybe I had learned something from my first year of teaching

The dancing made me feel both powerful and socially ostracized at the same time. I felt powerful while I was onstage, but unempowered and unacceptable when I wasn't. It had all become a drug: the attention, the music, the atmosphere, the fast money. I was somewhat addicted to it. The teaching demanded even more: time, patience, dealing with frustrations, having to toe the line and kiss ass. Yet it didn't give me any sense of power, or provide me with a sense of belonging; I had felt like an outsider teaching in Michigan. Part of me felt like I did belong at the club. The music was there, the stage was there, I knew the people there, and I could pretty much count on getting both money and attention while I was there. That's belonging. But it's an ephemeral vacuum that sucks the life out of a girl after a while.

It became more difficult for Pete to deal with the dancing as time went on. I kept telling him it wouldn't be much longer. Besides, he was in debt. So not only did he have a problem with it, he also felt powerless to stop it because of his financial position, which made him feel worse. He would have to deal with it or lose me. It was fast becoming a battle of wills: he wouldn't put a ring on my finger until I quit, but I wouldn't quit till he put a ring on my finger. Until there was a ring, I had no tangible assurance that he would follow through on his marriage intentions.

Another small problem was that he had found a few business cards I had saved from men I had met at the club. He found this disconcerting, even though I had told him they were only business associates who might be of use in the future. And that was the truth. But he didn't buy it. It was a chink in his armor.

35. CIRCLES

By the end of the summer, I finally got a job offer from a school in Torrance. It would be ninth- and tenth-grade English again, but a different syllabus. The school was in a decent area, and I liked the faculty I had met. However, the administration informed me that I would be using three different classrooms for some sort of spatial reasons. Not looking a gift horse in the mouth, I began preparing my lesson plans as soon as I got the news and tried to build positive momentum all summer. I had high hopes that the teaching job would work out, but still had a bad taste in my mouth from the first year of teaching. The job might have been what Pete was waiting for—to see if I could hold a job before he decided to marry me. If I couldn't teach, there was only the dancing, and he wouldn't be able to stand that any longer.

The truth was I didn't have the patience to do a lot of one thing for a long time. I could do a lot of one thing for a short time or I could do a little of one thing for a long time. Pete had kept the same routine for years, and he expected me to conform to it. He knew that I didn't like the idea of being a full-time employee, and he thought that meant I was just lazy. But I needed a high degree of change and variety in my *daily* life or I got bored—and he perceived that as a lack of discipline. Was I just a restless soul who would never be satisfied? Highly likely.

I loved theater and dance, and he knew it, yet he never offered to take me to these events. He didn't understand how my producing another show would "help" me. It would help me because it was what I loved. Whenever I talked about doing something like that in the future, he got irritated. If I talked about anything other than building a financial future, he would walk out of the room. I knew I wanted to be a performer and an artist, but I just didn't know how to do it successfully. And how could I justify it given our financial situation?

His daughter-in-law listened to me at the softball game as I told her how I felt about Pete's constant work, exhaustion, and stress level. She totally understood and spoke very objectively about what he really needed to do: file bankruptcy and start over. His work schedule had taken a toll on his previous marriage, and it must have been tough on his previous girlfriend as well. The truth was, he wasn't working for "us," he was struggling to pay off his divorce and child support, and to avoid the black mark of bankruptcy at all costs.

He was stubborn and his pride would kill him—like someone else I knew. He would not change for me, yet he expected me to quit dancing. It didn't seem worth it to wait ten years or more for us to build a house on the farm and to cut off all my options in the meantime.

When I realized I could make money dancing, all sorts of possibilities opened up. How could I give up the one thing that opened up my world? It may have been true that I was thirty-three, had no assets, and had more debt than income, but he was fifty-two with no assets, a family history of heart disease, and even more debt. I couldn't feel certain that he could provide me with a secure future, so I had to make sure I could continue to take care of myself somehow, no matter what.

The first day of school, I found out how hard it would be to race between three classrooms. The five-minute transition time left me breathless. I was the new kid on the block, so I was the one to get pinballed around. At least two of the rooms were across from each other. But the situation did not lend itself to my feeling like I had a home there. My "office" was in a storage room.

Torrance, California, was on a higher socioeconomic level than my hometown, and *most* of the kids came from more civilized homes. I had a class right after lunch, however, that was composed of twenty boys and four girls; it was by far the most challenging of all my classes. Knowing this would be the case, the first month I wore fake glasses and frumpy clothes to class. It didn't help. The boys had fun trying to get my attention, disrupt class, and distract me to the best of their ability. Yet I liked them, in a totally platonic way.

I learned from them. And they may have actually learned something from me. As we studied *Animal Farm*, the principal came in to evaluate me, and they amazed me. They behaved and even seemed absorbed in the story.

One November weekend, I was doing some organizing and cleaning. Pete had gone to a NASCAR race in Arizona with his sons. As I was moving a few things, I checked to see if anything had fallen behind the sofa. A large item was back there. I fished it out. It was a tape recorder. It was warm. It was plugged into the outlet and into the phone jack.

The tape had a recording of his last girlfriend's conversations on one side and mine from the day before on the other. So I spent the night with good company. It seems that she had generally the same experience with him that I did. And the broken record played on. He did not trust me and probably never would.

I called his ex-girlfriend in the morning and let her know that certain phone conversations of hers had been recorded. She confirmed that her experience with Pete had been pretty much the same as mine. But she had moved on and found satisfaction with another man and was the happy mother of a little girl. She wished me luck with Pete.

Why was her call still on the other side of the tape? Did he want to wallow in self-pity forever? And make others feel sorry for him too? But why should I? He brought on his own problems. He thought it was noble to let people walk all over him. It's not. It's pathetic. It was clear that there was no trust between us, and so I had to get out of there that very weekend. I packed everything and was ready to shove off by the time he came home.

At around one in the morning, he leaned over me and woke me with a kiss. I sighed and rolled away from him.

"Sweetheart, what's wrong?"

"I found the tape recorder."

He was silent for a moment.

"It was the only way to find out if I could trust you."

"You don't trust me and you never will, because of my job."

Always shying away from confrontation, he left the room and slept on the sofa that night. He was gone when I woke up. I made some calls, found an apartment in Torrance, loaded the car, and was off on my own again.

Of course, this personal drama affected my professional demeanor to a degree. But that was not the reason they didn't keep me on at Torrance. After working extremely hard to make the best of my situation, I was told that my classroom management skills were not up to par and that maybe I "wasn't suited for teaching." But then I met the teacher whose name I had seen written on boxes in one of the classrooms. She was in the district office when I was there one day, and she told me she had tried teaching in Huntington Beach for a year and found the place too "laissez-faire." She had tenure and was returning to Torrance to reinstate her position, which I had so tenaciously held for her in her absence.

Scared and lonely, I wound up calling Pete again. We got back together, and he actually proposed on New Year's Eve 2000 at the Charthouse in Malibu. We set the date for May 2001.

I wanted the wedding on the farm, since our agreement was to move to Michigan in a few years and fix up the old cabin. No matter how nice the weather, paying exorbitant rent in Southern California was just not worth it. Or so I believed.

36. BE CAREFUL WHAT YOU WISH FOR

It was Memorial Day weekend, and it had rained the entire week prior. We had a huge tent set up in a hayfield, with a dance floor even. And catering. But no amount of outdoor activity influenced the clouds overhead. It was fifty degrees and windy. The sides of the tent flapped in the wind as my brother scurried about trying to batten down the hatches with eyebolts. Pete even got up that morning to help try to mitigate the mud. Sawdust didn't help. Laying down boards didn't work. The dirt driveway to the field that had been used only by tractors and the stray pickup was nothing but deep, squishy mud. Getting guests to the site required a four-wheel drive.

Then there was me in a white wedding dress and white shoes. My uncle carried me from the vehicle to the soaked, matted, uneven red carpet. I carried my shoes and tiptoed up the mat to meet my dad outside the tent. The wind almost blew my headpiece off, but I was still pristine as I peered into the tent to get a glimpse of my niece as the flower girl.

Then it was our turn. My father lurched with me across the uneven mat toward the trellis he had made out of mulberry wood and which my mother had decorated with a bit too much zeal. The stroke had ruined his left leg, and it was a painful walk for him. He was self-conscious about it, looking down at his feet as he tried not to lose his balance. While steadying my father, I stared wide-eyed at the trellis as if it were some type of alien life form. The ribbons and fake flowers and nondescript greenery were dangling from every level and angle, almost obscuring the woodwork itself.

The sun made one fleeting appearance just as Pete was saying his vows, which he wrote himself. He said something about cloudy days and bright sunny days just as the sun peeked through the clouds for an instant.

His whole family was there, and the place impressed them as they gathered down by the pond for a few photos. His son told me that pictures did not do the place justice. We took them on a tour of the old cabin, too, laughing about how much work we would have to do. I had already drawn up a projected budget for what it would require.

After the ceremony, too many pictures were taken, not enough dancing took place, and it seemed that my brother's kids (he had three by then) and the dog upstaged everything else. Pete and I tried out our newly learned dance steps, but he had forgotten most of them. People stayed in spite of the cold, probably for the food. And that was my one wedding that took place outside a county clerk's office.

I had cajoled him into taking a cruise along the Inside Passage of Alaska, and the only way I got my way was by using *my* credit card. I just wanted to go somewhere untrammeled, somewhere pristine. Then I had to fight for an eleven day cruise instead of the seven day cruise he wanted, since I knew a week was just not enough for that place and all of its possibilities, but he was stressed about being gone from work so long. We flew to Anchorage and took a train to the Denali Lodge with a view of Mt. McKinley. We stayed up all night watching the sun "set" on one side of the peak and then "rise" on the other side about thirty minutes later, as the clouds rolled away to reveal the peak in full. We had the chance to take a plane trip from Talkeetna over the mountain, since we were blessed with beautiful weather in late June. I was able to get up close and personal with my Canon as we swept past the very top of the mountain.

The cruise set sail from Seward, AK for the Inside Passage, and we hit all the hot spots of Ketchikan, Skagway, and Juneau—taking the White Pass train and riding horses in Skagway, and being air lifted up to the top of a glacier in Juneau. I became acquainted with crampons and crevasses. The voyage steered near all the major glaciers, and we heard the thunder of "calving" as huge chunks broke off and we watched them melt as if they were sitting in a hot tub. The water was an absolute mirror as our vessel glided on the sky, slipping silently through the pristine reflection. I fell down on the bed and wept. It was a vision of infinity that left a permanent impression.

Then the honeymoon was over. We were back in Seal Beach, California, and I was still myself, yet trying to keep those images in my mind's eye. Even though I was married, I was still a wolf. I had to try to reconcile the two states of being. Putting on a public act had become onerous, and unfortunately, marriage puts people more in the public eye. That was another reason I had avoided it. It was like finally coming out of the closet of singlehood, dressed all in white, and taking vows that are impossible to fathom in front of everyone—*announcing* it to the world.

I just didn't feel the need to write any more announcements.

37. REAL LIFE

Ultimately, I had to deal with finances. I was planning on being poor my whole life, so what was my problem? On the farm, the money problems seemed to fade away; they were obscured by the trees. I felt so much at home there that any amount of debt just didn't seem like enough to ruin that feeling.

Pete didn't know that feeling. All he felt were the eyes of my dad upon him. I just ignored my father's negativity and insulated myself with the things I loved—powerful shields against anything the screwed-up world or parents could dish out.

By late July, I again managed to snag a part-time teaching gig at a Jewish school for girls in Culver City, for a staggering $15,000 salary. I took whatever I could get at that point. Since the girls had their religious studies in the morning, it would just be noon to five each day, so at least I would not have to force myself into morning mode. They signed me on to teach history and English, so I had an opportunity to relearn everything I had forgotten from sixth and seventh grade. The academic studies took place in modular trailers, while the more important religious teachings took place in an actual brick-and-mortar building.

Setting to work, I made classroom management first and foremost, making posters that outlined behavioral expectations and the like. They made me turn in lesson plans each week that had to follow the textbook exactly. There was a dress code for teachers—long skirts, legs covered, hair up—and the girls wore uniforms. The girls seemed nice and friendly at first, but they gradually showed me that they were in charge. After all, I was not Jewish; I was just a guest. There were other non-Jewish teachers there, but not many. Those girls were bright, stubborn, and very *very* accustomed to getting their way.

Then came the end of the world—September 11th. That morning, Pete's brother had called and told him to turn on the TV, and he turned on the small one in the bedroom and woke me up. We tuned in just before the second plane approached the tower. At first it was puzzling and didn't seem like any immediate emergency to me; I just sat in bed and watched as the smoke rose from the first tower. Then the second plane hit, and that was when I jumped out of bed and ran up to the screen. Oh. My. God. Within minutes it looked like the walls were tumbling down, as they showed footage off the street.

Were we under attack? Who did this? They kept running the footage again and again and then showing huge chunks of the towers raining down and the white and black smoke filling the streets and the general pandemonium that ensued. It was looking like Armageddon. National leadership and what Bush would do about this was my next concern.

I called the school, and they said not to come in that day. Pete left for work. Nothing kept him away from his auto shop. I stayed glued to the TV all day.

There was a meeting at the school the next day. They had decided it was best to act normal and not discuss the incident. These were sheltered kids, and they were not exposed to much media in their homes. So we pretended all was fine and went on with our daily rituals. The girls had also been told not to talk about it.

They went right on having fun, explaining all the rules and rituals that orthodox Jews had to follow. I just listened and nodded. When I told one of the geniuses in the class that I was from a farm, she offered a sympathetic "That's OK." Another invited me to her bat mitzvah in Beverly Hills, and I accepted. The place was a palace, and I hesitated to darken the massive double doors. They danced in an opulent ballroom with marble floors for hours, and they made me join in, which I did, awkwardly.

In the weeks following the 9-11 calamity, there were arguments, rushes to judgment, and constant coverage, to the point where I couldn't watch anymore. Afghanistan, al-Qaida, Iraq, Osama, the Taliban, Saddam Hussein... Then it was determined that we were going into Iraq to go after Saddam Hussein, even though everyone had agreed that Osama was in Afghanistan. I was dumbfounded. The most horrific attack had occurred, and so many people had died or would die from it. That was the most painful thing. The second most painful thing was that leadership appeared to be lacking. The third most painful thing was having to constantly hear the voice of President Bush.

Meanwhile, Pete actually expected me to get a tan, have my nails done, put on makeup, and dress up like a paper doll. Not gonna happen! That was not going to change the state of the world at the time. Why should I have to do all that *work*? I had *real* work to do. I was researching what was actually at the root of the attack.

He obviously thought I looked like crap without makeup and never would have even looked at me if I hadn't been wearing makeup when we met. I couldn't help it that he thought I was supposed to look like I did the day he met me. He didn't look the same. But that's OK. He's a *guy*. Women are judged by their looks. Period. For their entire lives. Men are only judged on income and wealth. And he wondered why I had spent over $2000 in the last six months on skin care? That was nothing. No one can kill time; time kills us. It's the ultimate consumer.

They did not renew my contract at the Jewish school. Imagine that. At that salary level, I couldn't even afford to keep working there. So I simultaneously set out to get both an acting agent and a teaching job. Whichever came first, I figured that was what I was meant to do.

That summer I found an agent showcase in Huntington Beach and actually had my own monologue ready to go. And I got an agent, even after handing her one of the headshots from 1995. The seven school districts to which I applied all said they were not in need of English teachers at the time. So there was the answer I had been looking for.

I had an agent and my course was finally set! I was excited again. I went out on auditions right away, and found a part-time job tutoring Chinese kids. Things were looking up.

38. TAPPING AT MY CHAMBER DOOR

I'd been at war for years…

rebelling against everything—

Against my dad.

Against society.

Against men.

Against my body.

The cancer was the embodiment of the war.

It was the belief that it's me

—alone

against the world.

Where was the unity? Where was the peace? It wasn't in me. Something malignant was in me. It had been slowly invading my pelvis for the last seven years since it had first been ferreted out in 1996. My periods had gotten very heavy and then simply ceased, and I thought my other ovary had just gotten "tired", so I didn't think it was any reason to see the doctor.

Six months later, I showed up for my regular annual pelvic exam, and she was concerned when I informed her of this perceived menopause. She found a basis for the concern as she poked around and felt a mass, and immediately sent me for an ultrasound. The pictures of the kids in her exam room laughed at me as I staggered around getting my clothes back on.

The ultrasound technician was rather cold. After the images were captured, she told me to get dressed, and she left the room. Lying there alone, I wondered what the images showed. She had hardly made eye contact with me. I tiptoed over to where she was hiding and asked if I could see the pictures. She just said the doctor would look at them and call me. Still no eye contract. I crept back over and peeked at the monitor myself, and there were just a lot of red lines going every which way. Were these blood vessels feeding the tumor? I choked back tears and terror.

"What is all that?!" I wailed.

She came back in the room. "That's just blood vessels. Don't worry, the doctor will call you."

I wept all the way home and stumbled up the stairs to the empty condo, where I threw myself on the bed, sobbing to Pete that I was sorry. I called him at work, where he always was.

The next day we went in to see the doctor to have her break the news to us in person. I needed a total hysterectomy. Right away. And probably chemo after that. There were two tumors, one on the back of the uterus and the other was the left ovary itself. Pete was stoic, and I fell apart. Then I had to call my agent. After having just gotten started again, this was rather crushing, as I would probably be losing my hair. Then there was my mother, whom I begged to be with me after the surgery. She promised she would.

It was six weeks before they could get me into surgery. This wasn't like booking a hotel room; it was like trying to get tickets to a sold-out show. And all that time I thought I was inching closer to death as the cancer cells spread to parts unknown. My mind turned into a dark tunnel with no light at the end of it. Sleeping became impossible, and my husband did not curl up with me; there was no spooning.

I felt I was just a whining child who was crumbling. The tutoring job at least kept me going out the door three days a week, but eventually I had to tell them I would be out of commission for a week or so.

When I finally got in for the procedure, Pete went into the pre-op dressing room with me, and we were singing that line from "The Crystal Ship" by The Doors: "Before you slip into unconsciousness, I'd like to have another kiss." I was scared. More like terrified. But while being wheeled into the operating room, I managed to smile and say something silly to the doc after he identified me as "the granulosa cell." He told me more about my chosen cancer cells: they grow in the connective tissue of the ovary. Good to know. Then tears rolled down the sides of my head as they transferred me onto the operating table under the bright lights. Those must be the lights that people talk about after they come back from the other side.

Pete went to the airport, picked up my mother, and brought her to the hospital. So they were both there when I was wheeled back to my room after a two-hour surgery. When I regained consciousness, the doc came around. He told me that it was stage two, and they had to take everything, including part of the lining of the stomach—a part called the omentum—and had removed dozens of lesions from the surface of the sigmoid colon. He thought six rounds of taxol would be effective, even though this cancer was so rare that this protocol was still just a best medical guess, according to scant research.

The good news? It had stayed within the pelvic cavity and had not spread to the lymph nodes. There was still hope for me. Then they stuck a patch on my stomach—estrogen—so I would not get osteoporosis at forty and might still have a normal sex life, for a while at least. They made me get out of bed the second day; it was good to get moving they said, helps the healing process. But the pain was ridiculous. Please more morphine.

After getting back to the condo, there was nothing but the slow crawl towards recovery, with nothing much to look forward to except the rounds of chemo. And trying to recover from the utter shock of knowing I actually had cancer after all the attention to exercise and nutrition and the avoidance of smoking, drinking, and pollution.

Mom stayed for three weeks. Pete slipped in and out without a word, and that made me more sad, and sadness made it harder to get well. He only worried about money. Why couldn't we be happy regardless of financial status or this disease? For better or worse? Why do we allow our attitudes to be affected by things that are so ephemeral? I felt alone. I didn't need that much of his time or money, but I needed his energy. I needed joy and creativity. I needed him to help me *keep hope alive*.

Didn't he want to help me recover? Did he believe in me? Did he want me to go away? I started to feel like the ultimate burden, and that was one thing I did not want to be—ever. Maybe there really isn't any such thing as love. Can its existence be proven? We live in a world that only seems to value what it can measure. So why do we fixate on love? Actually only the movies focus on love; the real world is focused on survival.

As I did battle with this uncommon type of cancer, I contemplated the notion of my own mortality. It's hard to imagine the world or the future without your own existence in it being a given. I scanned the horizon, searching in vain for meaning and assurances of something that allowed me to believe that if I did die in the next few years, my life had some small ripple effect in the ongoing stream of human consciousness. Was it a strong ripple? Would it send a message in a bottle to the shore? Or would my messages be left floating in the open sea, to be bandied about by the occasional pirate?

Humans simply do not look like they belong on the face of the planet. We just don't blend in very well. We forget that we are just another species, just another step on the ladder of evolution, not the whole show, not the epitome. We forget that many other species have been here much longer than we have, and they are so advanced that we can't understand them. And since we can't understand them, we assume we are superior to them. We do so much work for no better reason than to have the most advanced vehicle for our puny, peaked bodies.

It was just—

being so tired

and wanting to hide.

watching *Out of Africa*

over and over.

not wanting to be seen,

not wanting to see,

but trying to see anyway.

Communing with my computer.

And I used to be a dancer.

I never wanted to be on display again.

Pete worked all the time and it was my fault.

No money, no hair, gaining weight.

I was sick of that tea.

Real world speaking to female writer:

"Puh-leeze—we don't care about your sniveling, self-absorbed whining, nor do we want to listen to your far-left political diatribes. We don't care what you think, because you don't even count. Do you own any real estate? No? Then shut the hell up. Nothing matters in the real world except who you know, what you make, and what you've got. Well?"

The eyes of the world became a gunpoint. They burned into me like I was some sort of pathetic alien. But then, I'd always known that I was a foreigner in my own country anyway. Every day I would stand on the balcony of the condo and run my fingers over my balding scalp and watch the strands blow away, catching the sunlight as they flew. Good material for birds' nests. Were it not for medical technology, I would have been dead by then, at the ripe age of thirty-seven. Too much thinking. Too much time on my hands.

Death? Ha! Taxes? Not me. Kids? No way. I spent my life running from inevitability. Dad once told me, "You can't rebel against everything." Well, he did, and I certainly tried. Isn't cancer the ultimate rebellion? It's a bunch of rebel cells doing things they're not supposed to do. Mutants. The fact that this cancer started in the very organs that made me female led me to hypothesize that some part of my subconscious was indeed rebelling against being female. And isn't that the area of the body where anger comes from?

I became a ghost of my former self, no longer having the strength, the drive, or the vision of my youth. Reading my old writing was the only way to get a glimpse of all that. Then I'd just laugh. Pete seemed to be something of an apparition as well. He would just tiptoe in, make a bit of cheese and beer disappear, float in and out of the shower, melt into the sofa, and finally vaporize into bed. In the morning, there was barely a trace of him.

But in the end, what really matters is making sure that your life makes a good movie. Because when you look back, you don't want to have boring memories. All you wind up with is memories, after all. If you have a memorial of some sort and people show up, above all, they should not be bored. Some people remember with things, others remember with words, images, or music. These are all tips of icebergs that go deep and are mostly hidden. But it's all about keeping memories alive, and that is a chore for the survivors.

39. BALD

Pete drove me to the chemotherapy sessions, but it was hard for him to take the time away from his auto shop. He was always under stress. As he was bending over tying his shoes one morning before we left, I mused aloud that this all must be some sort of test. He stated, "Yes, it's a test of my commitment to you." There was something about his tone of voice and lack of eye contact that told me he was failing this test—and that he knew it. He nodded off during the sessions as I sat there with the IV in my arm. Good times.

The wig I found worked pretty well. My students could not tell anything different, but I think they knew something was a bit off. Yet as polite Chinese children, they never asked me if I was wearing a wig. They kept me going in their own sweet way, and I was actually lucky, because I don't think I could have handled a regular classroom of thirty kids at the time. Not becoming distracted with my medical status was a monumental effort for poor pitiful me. But the small tutoring business closed up shop a few months later, and that summer I wound up unemployed.

Pete blamed me for everything about my situation and so did my dad. So it was no wonder that I sat around and figured out how everything was my fault, even the cancer.

I knew from the start of my dance degree that I would never have a high level of financial or emotional stability, but I abhorred the prospect of relying on anyone for anything. So staying on the farm or marrying some rich guy were not things I even contemplated, except under extreme duress. Those arrangements were akin to clinging to someone while rearranging the deck chairs on the Titanic. Teaching high school was probably not the right field for me, but I had to try to stay in the field because it was the only profession in which I had any qualifications. If I tried to branch out and take some classes in other subjects, Pete told me I was chasing dreams again.

So we had many lovely evenings of crying and fighting.

I didn't know how the arrangement was going to work, because he *did* expect me to work; he just wouldn't come out and *say* it. If I couldn't find a decent job, what else was there to do besides go to school of some sort? I put a scarf over my bald head and pounded the pavement. I went everywhere looking for work, but found nothing. Not even

McDonald's would take me on. I must have looked like a homeless woman.

I tried to stop thinking about the end of my life. I'd be OK, I told myself. But what was another twenty or thirty or forty more years? There is never enough time. How long, doc? How long have I got? When do I find out the test results? When do I need more tests? When will I need surgery again? Will there be some better treatments out soon? *Did I cause this?* Was it the chemicals in the beauty products and all the containers of hope and preservatives out there? Was it the stress? But I did yoga for god's sake. Or Buddha's sake. Or for my own sake. Was it the unprotected sex with two guys in my twenties? It had been only two; after the abortion I was adamant about condoms. Or maybe it was linked to the abortion, which was perhaps linked to the pelvic infection, which in turn became the cancer. Was it because my periods had started early and there were no breaks because there were no pregnancies? Maybe it was all the tofu and soy milk I had consumed, like my dad had postulated. At the time, I did not know anything about the phytoestrogenic aspects of soy or why I had to worry about any such thing. *Oh yes, surely all my fault*.

So I needed to repent and never have sex again? Go to church? And then I would be happy and be forgiven for my horrible hormone-driven transgressions in my twenties? That all sounded like a very convenient *un*truth. It was all just the luck of the draw, bad timing, and poor circumstances. I knew there were women out there who were far more sexually active than I had been. Why me? Not everyone has these problems...

40. DELIVERANCE

2004 was a year of reckoning. I decided I had to stop living a financial lie, the teaching job was not emerging, my writing wasn't about to sell anytime soon, and my acting career was DOA. First, I got rid of the credit cards. *All* of them. I took the kitchen scissors and snipped each shiny, glittery, evil piece of plastic into five jagged pieces and dumped them in the wastebasket. I did this in front of my husband as he stared at me. Then I told him he should do the same thing, and that unless he gave me an allowance, I would not be able to both buy food and pay my own bills. So he agreed to give me $60 a week.

I had already talked to my dad about my financial situation and asked if he would consider sending me a little money each month, or even selling a few acres, just to help me through these difficult times. No, he could not. That would make him look bad. Besides, most of the net income from the family business had to go to my brother's family since he was doing the farming, and they had three kids and no other jobs. I guess my dad figured Pete would help me, that I really wasn't that bad off, and that I would somehow get back on my feet.

These facts about my brother and sister-in-law, however, were the root of growing resentment. After dropping out of the University of Michigan, the baby of the family had married a fundamentalist Baptist woman who had little education and no other goals in life except to have kids, go to church, and bake cookies. She believed this was the Lord's plan. My other brother was single and had no kids, and he seemed content to just work for my brother for little more than room and board. Something in the water I guess...

A month later, I decided to put my cell phone service on hold because gas prices were so high that I couldn't afford the $40 a month for anytime minutes anymore. I couldn't even afford to drive anywhere anyway, and the only time I needed my phone was when I was in the car. So it was back to e-mail and hearing Mom's voice only on the weekends.

Doing without credit cards and a constant cell phone heightened my awareness of the state of mind that I was in when I wished those things were there. With the cell phone, it was my need to hear another familiar voice whenever I felt the least bit lonely or if I had some existential question that I thought might flummox my mother. With credit cards, well, it was just the desire to eat. I had become an adult.

With all this financial morass going on, the 2004 election campaign was in full swing that summer, and I noticed an ad looking for street canvassers with the Democratic National Committee. That was it. I spent the summer pounding more pavement all over West Los Angeles, collecting funds to "Beat Bush," and earned a small commission that made me feel sort of viable again.

We went to all the farmers markets and were quite well received by the generally liberal population of Los Angeles County. Pete was very much aware of my political stance and had voted for Bush in 2000. He did not care much for political conversation with me, and I assumed this was because he knew I had more information on the issues and would of course try to prove myself correct. Arguments were great fun for me, as my dad and I had always had quite lively "debates" late at night in the kitchen. But Pete just walked out of the room if I brought up any points of contention.

Michigan was a swing state, so I flew home to vote there, and after the highly controversial results were in and I was done throwing an absolute fit, I called Pete. He went right ahead and told me he had voted for Bush. That landed with a thud that sounded like divorce papers in my brain. How could any person in the nation actually vote for that man? And I was married to one who did. And that was it. He had abandoned me emotionally after the cancer, he was a Bush fan, he would never get ahead, and I felt like a burden to him. Europe was looking better and better.

I dragged out the World Atlas and started charting my escape from America. I was back to my political bones, but felt America was not there for me anymore, and perhaps never was.

The road less traveled was certainly not paved with gold.

Hollywood didn't buy my script like they were supposed to, I had to dance for a bunch of drunks, and no one wanted me in the school system. So are the arts supposed to be relegated to the land of hobbies, like chess and cooking? Knowing it was hard was supposed to make me change my mind? That was giving up, and I couldn't give up. I could only take breaks, rethink my strategy, and try again. I had a few illusions and I was having a hard time parting with them. But it was all still better than taking the path of least resistance—if there ever was one.

And the whole time I just kept wondering why every endeavor was like banging my head against a brick wall. Would it have been easier if I were a man? Or born into a family that stayed in Boston and only had one child? Was life this hard for everyone? Or had I set my sights too high? How high is too high? Doesn't it depend on how low I am when I start?

After the election, I went back to California and got a job in a small Montessori preschool. It was an OK place, but not open to anything new. I was in charge of snack time, nap time, play time, and generally assisting as needed, for $9 an hour. But it was full-time and I made the best of it. I knew Pete and I were growing apart. We had not had sex in over a year. When we tried, it hurt, and we quit trying.

One night after another argument over leaving California for Michigan, he said he no longer wanted to go.

We finally decided on a divorce mutually—over the cell phone. I had just pulled into a parking space at Wild Oats, and the bottom of my world fell away again—on one gorgeous Southern California afternoon. When I called him, he already seemed completely resigned to it and didn't even want to make time to try to work it out. He had probably been seeing someone.

Somehow we managed to live together in a civil fashion until I scraped together enough money to leave. I had lost the drive to work in California, and if there's one thing you cannot lose in California, it's your *drive.* What was the point? The climate? I wanted to be back on the farm with my family. The cabin would never be fixed if I waited for him to come back with me.

After returning home from work one miserable day in February, I picked up the mail as usual and found an envelope from UBS addressed to me. Puzzled, I opened it, and there it was: a check for $10,000 from my aunt—my father's sister, whom he hated. She had passed in the December following the election. Divine mercy perhaps? She was my angel. At last I had a chance to strike out on my own. I could be free! I had been saving and saving, and credit was flowing well then. So I did the math and decided that I could leave in June.

Now there was light at the end of the tunnel. I even decided to join the Alumni Association of the University of Michigan, since they had a chapter in LA, and I just wanted to get out there a bit before heading back to the sticks. In the back of my mind, there was the outside possibility that I might meet someone more educated than my soon-to-be-ex-husband.

The alumni group was sponsoring a tour of downtown Los Angeles, partnering with the historical society, and I had never even been to downtown LA. So on a breezy day in early May, I waltzed out of the condo in Seal Beach and drove to downtown Los Angeles with an open heart and mind, and met my next husband-to-be that very day.

41. CATCH AS CATCH CAN

Gliding through the gilded doors of the Biltmore Hotel, I found the gray-haired ladies with the historical society gathered for the tour, chatting amongst themselves, and a tall guy who did not seem to fit in. He walked like a duck and quacked like a duck, so I knew he was a sitting duck, and quite an animated one at that. Reading men had become an ingrained skill.

Frank was bald, tall, and rotund, with rather large eyes, and looked like he was approaching sixty. He noticed me immediately as I tried to be friendly by commenting to the group, "Do you all know each other?" They laughed and said no. Frank sidled up to me and promptly started unloading all sorts of unnecessary backstory and trivia, making a glaring attempt to seem hyper-intelligent and sophisticated. Unfortunately, he came off as a bit clownish.

He was excited to broadcast the news of his recent purchase of a loft in one of the downtown warehouse conversions and obviously thought this was a major selling point of his. I was somewhat dubious. I informed him I was about to drive back to Michigan to renovate an old cabin, and this did not impress him that much. But it apparently represented a distinct challenge. So he blathered on about himself in that way men do when they think they are a catch and must try to convince the available woman at hand of this fact.

This shallow behavior is based on the usual assumptions, primarily the assumption that the single woman is always looking for a "catch". Maybe she isn't! And men certainly cannot be the judge of whether or not they are indeed a catch, as every woman has a different definition of a catch. Men have the false belief that all women are looking for money, but no amount of money can create compatibility. She might be looking for some short-term fun that costs money, and he may be looking for the same thing. Who knows? And does this even matter?

After the tour and listening to his nonstop chatter, he walked me back to my car and paid for my parking. Funny how I never seem to carry any cash.

The truth is, divorced, wealthy, and/or ambitious men are a lot more wary about women they hook up with these days, and as they age, there is even less reason to get married. The same can be said for women. Any and all negative experiences with the opposite sex in the past make mature people less likely to put up with anything. A bigger tax deduction? The same sex every night? Yawn.

What exactly is this vapor that arises from a mix of plain old hormones, old-fashioned notions, and bald-faced lies invented by Madison Avenue and Hollywood? Nothing is really sacred when it comes right down to it. Just watch *Seinfeld*. Bubbles are bursting all over America right now, but somehow there is always another one being inflated. There's a gigantic bubble machine behind that curtain.

The first time I had dinner with Frank, I was caught off-guard as he reached across the table and took my hand. I knew he was needy, but this was too much. He was kind of a fun guy; he liked to drink and laugh, he was well-educated and well-read, he owned his home, and he was in fairly good shape financially. And we had both graduated from Michigan. But we were seventeen years apart in age, and I was just not physically attracted to him. I had also decided that marriage should not be an act of charity or pity, for either party. Eventually a woman realizes that hot sex is not as long lasting or as important as a house and financial security, but what fun is life without hot sex? It's like a trade-off for keeping an old guy company.

But who really wants to make those compromises, even if they might seem to make life easier? No one wants to be in a needy or dependent position. Living alone is a great thing if the alternative is living with someone who makes you feel like your life is over. Is it a cop-out to marry an older needy guy for increased financial security? Or is it a job description? Due to the demographics of the nation, most guys are at least ten years older than I am. Can I help it if this is the fish bowl from which I have to fish? Or maybe I should just give up fishing, what with all the baiting, outfitting, and waiting—and disappointment when the fish just isn't acceptable.

Following our first meeting, the stream of phone calls and e-mails from him was endless. We had lunch a few times, and I was counting the days to my departure. There were some twinges of guilt, since I was still living with my soon-to-be ex-husband, but we were sleeping apart, and we rarely spoke or even saw each other.

Since I had been starved out and needed some extra cash for the trip home, I went back to my old entertainment venue to gather some extra funding, and when Pete got wind of this, the divorce papers appeared. We agreed that he would pay me a bit of alimony for a year, ship my stuff back to Michigan, and give me a small amount of the bond fund his aunt left him a few years earlier, about $4000. It was fair enough after only a four-year marriage. In aggregate, I was going back to Michigan with a scintillating $20,000! To me, that was a princely sum. I knew I would need all of it and more in order to Cali-fornicate that 1950s cabin in the woods.

When the day of departure arrived, I sat on the sofa in what had been my makeshift home office and contemplated what I was about to do. I knew there was no other option at that point but to walk out the door, but I was leaving a comfortable condo in California to go to a cabin in the woods of Michigan that was unlivable at that time. And my dad would be there, making everything even more difficult. But I could not stay in a loveless marriage for climate, high-speed internet, and cable. It would have been OK if I had been living with a roommate and had a job, but that was not the case. It really came down to not having a job or much of a marriage either. And there was something about that cabin.

I figured I had some time to find a health insurance plan and get some type of job to pay for it. After all, divorces take forever in Orange County, California. Maybe I would even have to dance again, but not until after I fixed my cabin. It had become my embryo and I could not think beyond the birthing process. After staring at my Sierra Club posters on the wall for over an hour, I commenced dismantling my Southern California existence, carefully packing my little red Civic hatchback with all my cherished belongings.

When I was finally finished, I got in the car and sat on my red-striped seat covers for another few moments of reflection as a sense of dread and self-doubt settled into the pit of my stomach. What was I doing? Where was I really headed? And most importantly, did I have enough money to get me wherever it was I thought I needed to go?

At his insistence, I drove to Frank's apartment in Hollywood. His new loft would not be ready to move into for several months. He was a happy puppy dog at my arrival, like he had waited a long time for a playmate. But when he had me sit on his lap and watch online porn, I was completely turned off. Yes, I had mentioned my brief foray into the adult industry, but this felt lewd and completely inappropriate. He apologized, but he had become even more unattractive to me by that point. We shared a bed together, but I did not allow sex. I shoved off early the next morning. He watched me go with his sad clown face.

All across the country, he called me every few miles to check on my progress. He tracked me at work on the computer. It was overkill, and I finally had to turn the phone off. It seems that some people need constant contact. Not me. State after state went by as I tried to feel young and free-wheeling again, but it was fleeting. I knew what a daunting task I had in front of me. My dad would make things as pain-staking as possible. I had a list and a budget for the project, but I knew that each item would be a fight. He knew I had his sister's money, and he had to feel guilty, since he never gave me as much as she did. Or maybe not.

42. FULL CIRCLE

It was finally time to make the cabin my own, like I had dreamed of doing since 1984 when I left for Ann Arbor. It had been sitting there waiting for me to return ever since. The knotty-pine walls were in good shape, the pine floors were worn like an old dance studio, and the moldy shingle roof had been replaced with a green, galvanized metal roof in 2001. It had heard the spring peepers and withstood the rain, wind, and blizzards, and with its two big windows in the front facing the highway, it had watched many a truck go by on its way to where I probably was.

The structure sat in a small woods, and was just far enough back from the highway as to be inconspicuous to drivers, yet close enough so that any occupants in the cabin could faintly hear the traffic. I felt like a bird snug in my cozy nest, hearing and watching traffic go by, but knowing I was hidden from view, at least in the summer.

I saw myself as the savior of the little cabin by the side of the highway in a patch of Michigan woods.

My dad and I forgave each other as we went shopping for yards and yards of electrical wire, much of which is still in the basement of the cabin. His stroke had left its mark on the left side of his face, and he still could not quite close his left eye. They had placed a gold weight in it to help it close. Regardless of the pain it caused him, he was determined to make sure that all the work on the cabin was done in-house. It was to be him, me, or my brother who would do it all.

Since the overhead electrical wire had been taken out in a storm a decade earlier, we dug a trench for the underground electrical line. I had to use the shop vac to get the clods of dirt out of the trench so it would be the requisite six feet deep. It was ominous, odious work. Then we had to tell the raccoons and squirrels to take a hike, which meant sealing up the attic. This my father did on his back. Then we commenced with the windows and the electrical work.

Dad went up and down the basement steps, dragging his bad leg. He had to pause for breath at the top step. I kept telling him that my brother could do it or I could get some guy from Lowe's. No, that was not allowed. We made a rough opening in the attic and took in forty sheets of drywall before installing the semi-circle window he had been saving for many moons.

This work all happened between July and October 2005, as I was pushing to get it done before the snow flew. My dad chose the wrong sealant for the floor in the bedroom and it never cured, so I set to work on my hands and knees scraping and sanding to get the goo off the floor. In the meantime, Dad and I moved my bed into the dining area in front of the window, so I could at least start spending the night in the cabin. The first morning I woke up surrounded by yellow maple leaves trying to get a good view of what was happening inside the cabin.

Mom and Dad then struggled to get their previous, rusty, wood-burning stove into the basement. This was the stove that had valiantly attempted to heat the drafty farmhouse the whole time I grew up in it. I knew I was in for a long, cold winter. But it was my space—my tiny corner of the planet where I could feel somewhat safe and free.

While slaving away trying to get myself a livable place, Frank called me three times a day or more. My hands were full, while he had little to do, sitting at his office job all day. As I mopped the floor for the tenth time, the phone would ring, and there would be the voice saying, "I love you. I want to marry you." He was usually drunk. We had known each other three months, had been out a handful of times, and hadn't even had sex yet. I guess because he had seen my breasts, that was enough. He was sure that I was the one.

I just figured the guy was immeasurably lonely and bored. And I was on the fence as to whether I would go back to California or not. What would I do for work?

At last I moved in, just as the weather cooled considerably. I sat at my computer feeling the blood in my veins slowly congeal. After living in a warm climate for almost ten years, this process felt like a leaden weight pressing down on my bones. I figured the barometric pressure had to be to blame for the slow growth of the area. The "lake effect" was winter blues. I ran out to purchase full-spectrum bulbs and frequented the tanning salons, but this was a poor substitute for the Southern California sun beaming down every day.

Questioning the wisdom of my move, I began to think that maybe renting in a sunny climate was better than owning in dismal Michigan—if you can afford it. With renting, there's no worry about a mortgage, loss of value, endless maintenance costs, or eternal property taxes that may go up. It began to dawn on me that being rich was not about living in a castle in the south of France or driving a Ferrari on the Pacific Coast Highway. These things are just a big waste of space and fuel. Being wealthy was about having options, investing well, and maybe starting a business of one's own. The artist was finally starting to figure it out.

In March, while I was lying on my kitchen floor in a small pool of sunlight, Frank was waiting for the floor of his loft to be chemically stained so he could finally move in. I knew little about this process and thought it sounded cool. Little did I know the odor would linger for months. He kept me informed up to the minute as to the status of said improvements, since he was expecting me to take him up on his marriage proposal—I assumed. I was still concerned about my lack of income and what I would do for work once I got back to civilization. Just living off him was unacceptable.

Anxious to leave, yet reluctant to go, I wondered if I was being bought out. Was I just something pretty to add to the décor of new digs for a sixty-year-old hipster metrosexual? When he sent me his credit card in the mail, I was then under obligation to go. Did that put me in the driver's seat—literally? Or was I just a nifty new appliance being ordered from out of state?

The day I left (again) was rather off-key. I sprawled on the floor (again) and cried while my mom stood over me and told me that I didn't want to live in the cabin all by myself for the rest of my life. "Yes I do," I wailed. My father kept sitting down, getting up, pacing, sitting down again, and finally saying, "I gotta go," and exiting the scene. Eventually I got up off the floor and realized I had to go and give it a try. The cabin wasn't going anywhere, and I could always come back and cry on the floor whenever I felt like it in the future. I packed my Civic—again.

I drove around to the farmhouse to bid my parents good-bye again. My mother stood in the background as my father squinted at me through his one good eye and leaned against the car door.

"I don't know why you keep leaving like this," he said. "The next time you come back, we may not be here."

I hugged him. "Don't say that. You'll both be around for a long time still."

As I slowly drove out of the driveway and waved good-bye to my little cabin, I was overtaken with waves of grief, knowing that he may be right. The piercing shards of the realization that someday the whole place might not even be there rained down on me. Once on I-80, I had to pull over twice as I was blinded by tears.

What would happen if they weren't there someday?

I had never even contemplated such a thing. They seemed like fixtures, rocks of Gibraltar.

Those words were indeed the last words he ever spoke to me. He had a massive coronary two months later while cutting down box elder trees. The question of whether or not he was trying to end it all that way, rather than in a hospital bed, remains for the survivors to ponder for the rest of their days.

He used to say, "The land is my soul," when speaking in that floating, idyllic mode in which mad scientists so often find themselves. Perhaps when one becomes so embedded in a place, he literally merges with it, unable to be transplanted, transported, or uprooted.

His ashes were scattered by the pond and behind the cabin. My mother is probably still hiding some in the farmhouse somewhere. After all, she wants to keep him in the house with her. These are his final resting places. My job now is to be the phoenix rising from the ashes—again.

43. BARE BONES

So, what is the meaning of all this? Such a good question and never for me to answer. Am I now free from having to prove something to my father? Can I now stop the patterns of trying to earn the approval I never got from him by gaining it from other men? Can I now stop listening to anyone who acts like I should have endless regrets when they don't even know me? Or is this a permanent condition of being unable to forgive him, all men, and all of society for having expectations of me that have nothing to do with who I really am?

Did I cast myself out or am I an outcast? Or am I casting about looking for my true home? And does this endless searching make me a castaway by its very nature? The soul does select her own society. And she does not want to be judged or dismissed for being what she is. And being who I am now, I would not even look twice at any of the men I have recalled. We go through inner evolutions and revolutions.

All through this life, like any life, there were unexpected turns, and there were stones that perhaps I should have left unturned. Then there were stones that tripped me up on my way to where I thought I wanted to go. Yet it is the falling down and the rising from the ashes that makes us who we are, or remakes us.

But still we wonder, "Is this the life I was supposed to have? Or did I miss the boat?" What is the life any woman is "supposed to" have? It is still hard to say, as men are still generally *assumed* to be capable of almost anything, but women must *prove* that they are capable. The bar is set very high right out of the box. True freedom for women will come when this bar is set at the same height for all and when we free ourselves from guilt, leave our comfort zones, and go out into the world at large to face all its unseemly contradictions and convolutions. Family is not the only important thing in life if it holds us back from realizing our true potential. And status is not gained through mere association, whether through birth or marriage.

In my fleeting arc of existence, driven solely by striving after the wind, I sought the truth hidden in the inner life of all things, taking nothing at face value, listening but not following, taking nothing for granted, and appearing supremely self-centered or completely liberated, depending on who is looking.

The truth from all of us collectively would be *the* truth. But we have yet to tell it, with no agendas. This is my letter to the world that may write back to me someday. I'll wait for the truth to come around, once it gets its boots on.

A TREE FELL

A tree fell in the woods...
and I finally heard it.
It seems the world has finally heard it.
My father knew that the road now most traveled
by the American economy
was the road to ruin.
And he would rant about this,
flailing his arms
like big branches in a stiff wind.
Nothing worked in his book
except work,
cold, hard manual labor.
And so he died working—
defending his woods from an invasive species.
The old box elders hit back,
and my father became part of the deep, dark,
and lovely woods—
the place he loved the most.

If a *woman* does not keep pace with her companions, perhaps it is because she hears a different drummer. Let her step to the music which she hears, however measured or far away.

—Henry David Thoreau
(with a few changes)